HOT SEAL, OPEN ARMS

A SEALS IN PARADISE NOVEL

TERESA REASOR

This is a work of fiction. Names, characters, places, and incidents are the product of the author's imagination or are used fictitiously, and any resemblance to actual persons, living or dead, business establishments, events, or locales is entirely coincidental.

HOT SEAL, OPEN ARMS
A SEALS IN PARADISE NOVEL

COPYRIGHT © 2022 by Teresa J. Reasor

All rights reserved. No part of this book may be used or reproduced in any manner whatsoever without written permission from the author, except in the case of brief quotations embedded in critical articles or reviews.

Contact Information: teresareasor@msn.com

E-book Edition Cover by Cat Johnson
Print Edition Cover by Cat Johnson and Tracy Stewart
Edited by Faith Freewoman

Teresa J. Reasor
PO Box 124
Corbin, KY 40702

Publishing History: First Edition 2022

ISBN 13: 978-1-940047-47-8
ISBN 10: 1-940047-47-1

Print Edition

TABLE OF CONTENTS

PROLOGUE 1
CHAPTER 1 5
CHAPTER 2 15
CHAPTER 3 27
CHAPTER 4 37
CHAPTER 5 47
CHAPTER 6 55
CHAPTER 7 67
CHAPTER 8 75
CHAPTER 9 87
CHAPTER 10 99
CHAPTER 11 107
CHAPTER 12 115
CHAPTER 13 123
CHAPTER 14 133
CHAPTER 15 143
CHAPTER 16 155
CHAPTER 17 165
CHAPTER 18 173
CHAPTER 19 183
More Information and Books by Teresa Reasor 191

INTRODUCTION

PROLOGUE

THE CHINOOK MOTOR'S high metallic whine chanted in unison with the staccato sound of blades cutting through the air above them.

Wyatt's attention moved restlessly about the fuselage as voices traveled above the hum. Wilder and Needles had a back-and-forth going. He couldn't hear the details, but based on Wilder's expression, Javier was living up to his nickname and needling him about something.

Thor was strapped into one of the seats, arms crossed, legs braced, taking a fifteen-minute power nap. The guy was unshakable and oblivious to the noise.

Stefan's Brooklyn-accented voice cut into Wilder and Javier's conversation as he joined them.

Bishop and Hogan seemed to be lost in their own thoughts while they waited.

The two SEALs who'd been tacked onto their team, Staples and Norman, sat together. The two earned their tridents six months before and were as yet untested in combat. Why on earth the head shed decided a rescue mission would be a good way for the two to bust their cherries made no sense. But to question that decision was way above Wyatt's pay grade.

"Ten minutes until the drop site," the pilot's voice came over the com system.

Wyatt withdrew the photo from one of his vest pockets and took a final look at the picture of the couple. He looked like an average guy, clean cut, early forties, doctor. She was a nurse and a looker. Dark hair, even features, pretty. He hoped that hadn't worked against her.

These people had to have balls of steel to travel to one of the most volatile countries in Niger on a humanitarian mission. The armed gangs and terrorists who ruled the country took hostages all the time...as Drew and Nancy Monahan recently learned the hard way. And now the team was going in to recover them. Hopefully in one piece.

The pilot's voice came over the com system. "Drop site in five."

Wyatt tucked the picture back in place.

Senior Chief Ramon's voice came through his com. "Fall in. Keep your spacing. You don't want to crowd the guy beside you." He'd be the one to call them off at the top of the ropes as they rappelled forty feet to the bottom on separate, side-by-side lines.

Wyatt put on his tactical gloves and fell in line. Senior Chief yelled out "*Go.*" Team Leader Stefan Kowalski and Thor hit the rope first. Ty and Mason went next, then Javier and Wilder. Banger stepped off with Norton the newbie, leaving Wyatt paired with Staples.

At Senior Chief's yell, Wyatt grabbed the line, pushed off, dropped beneath the Chinook, and started down. Even with his tactical gloves the friction of the rope heated his palms. He was aware of Staples' movements just above and to the left of him just before he left him behind.

Fifteen feet from the bottom, a disturbance of the air, a flash, a shadow bearing down on him on the left had him gripping the line hard. A body traveling at momentum struck his shoulder. The pain was sharp and deep, but he barely had a second to give voice to it before being ripped off the line.

The hard-packed desert rose up to meet him. He landed hard atop a body, his arm beneath him and yelped in pain as his elbow popped.

Sand whipped around him from the propellers of the Chinook blowing the particles into his face. Wyatt rolled off the man beneath him and cried out again when his arm flopped. He cradled it with his right hand to hold it in place and keep it stable.

"Easy, Rodeo. Just lie still." Kowalski hit his com button. "Staples fell and dragged Taylor off the line. We have two injured men and we need evac for both."

The Chinook banked and moved away.

Wyatt clenched his eyes shut and fought back a wave of nausea and the need to cry out with pain while Ty unbuckled the straps on his pack and slipped them off over his shoulders. At least having the weight of the pack off eased the pain and nausea—as long as he didn't move.

"Rodeo, I need you to answer some questions for me," Javier's voice dragged Wyatt's eyes open. The man was one of the best medics the team ever had.

"Did you hit your head or hurt your neck?" he asked while he was running his fingers down Wyatt's neck.

"No, but my arm feels like it's been ripped off."

Javier ran careful hands over his shoulder and elbow while Wyatt gritted his teeth against the agony of even that careful pressure.

"Your shoulder and elbow are dislocated, Rodeo, and I can't put them back in. It might cause more damage."

Javier was soft-pedaling it. Wyatt's arm felt like it wasn't even part of his body.

"I'm going to give you a shot of morphine to take the edge off."

Thank God. Gritting his teeth against the pain wasn't cutting it.

He barely felt the needle go into his arm. The meds hit his system, the agony eased, and he was able to turn his thoughts to something else. "Is Staples okay?"

"You slowed his fall, but he's broken his leg and he probably has a concussion."

"Better that than dying." Had the damn FNG fallen from thirty feet he'd never have survived. The sand in this dry African desert was packed like concrete.

"We're going to load you back on the Chinook and they're going to take you back to base for medical treatment. You're going to be okay."

"Fuck! What about the mission?" The Team would be going into the rescue two men short.

"It'll be okay, Rodeo," Mason said. "We got this."

He held onto that thought for the next five minutes while Javier stabilized his arm by wrapping it tight against his body. Ty and Thor put a splint on Staples' leg.

Ty got on the radio. The Chinook circled back and lowered a transport basket.

Strapped into the basket Wyatt let the morphine lull him. Ty gave his good shoulder a squeeze and yelled into his ear above the thunder of the chopper. "We'll see you when we get back to base, Rodeo."

"Watch your six," Wyatt said.

The world spun as the basket rose to meet the open side door of the chopper. Wyatt closed his eyes, the movement making him nauseous. The flight crew wrestled the basket inside and secured it to the bulkhead.

They lowered the next basket for Staples. Three minutes to load them, then the Chinook turned south back to base.

From beside him, Staples' voice came to him. "I'm sorry, sir."

"We're both going to come back from this, Staples." It was just a dislocated shoulder and elbow. He'd recover from these injures and be back with his team in a few months.

CHAPTER 1

Six months later

"WE'VE GONE AS far as we can with your treatment, Wyatt," Dr. Masters said.

Wyatt studied the man's expression and tried to look beyond the doctor's professional veneer. He had a long, thin face, a thick bush of hair, delicate, long-fingered hands, and looked down his nose every time he spoke.

Wyatt's arm and shoulder weren't even close to being back in working order. He had numbness in his hand and forearm. His shoulder was still giving him pain even though the surgery successfully repaired the torn rotator cuff and ligaments. But now there were other random symptoms he'd tried to ignore. Mentioning them had triggered this dialogue.

"We've taken every surgical avenue available to us to try and repair the damage to your elbow joint and the ulna nerve there. And we've seen some improvement, but the nerves aren't rebounding as we'd hoped."

"It sounds like you're backpedaling, Doc."

Masters looked off to one side instead of meeting his eyes.

Wyatt had known something was up when the doctor called and asked him to come to his office after his physical therapy session. And if calling him by his first name was meant to be comforting, fuck that. It wasn't working. "I want another surgeon and/or at least another opinion. We're talking about my career here, and the half a million dollars Uncle Sam shelled out to train me."

"We can't release you back to active duty, Petty Officer. There's no way you could deploy with your team."

Blocking off the stomach-cramping reaction he had to that last sentence, he drilled Masters with a narrow-eyed look. "Who's we?" he asked.

Masters blinked rapidly. "Me and doctor Sanderlin, the head of orthopedic surgery here at the hospital."

"Call Sanderlin up and ask him to join us. I want to hear what he has to say."

"Dr. Sanderlin just finished several surgeries today and has left the hospital."

He'd call the man up tomorrow and make an appointment to speak to him.

"We can give it a little more time and see how things go." Masters' tone remained even, but he again avoided meeting Wyatt's eyes. "You need to prepare yourself for the possibility that the nerves might never recover."

"I'm doing my PT and keeping the muscles in shape." But they weren't rebounding. His left forearm was odd-looking, smaller than his right, and the grip of his left hand was still weak. And he wasn't going to think about the numbness.

"It's been six months Wyatt. We'll ease into another six, but after that, if things don't improve, I'll have to recommend a medical discharge."

Fuck! The blow halted his breath. "After nearly ten years of service, I'm only worth six more months of your time, Doc?" he asked.

Doctor Masters' expression tightened. "Even my expertise has its limits, Petty Officer. You've paid a huge price because of an accident. But not as big a one as some I've operated on. You can still move on and have a productive life, Wyatt."

But not as a SEAL. And not as a man with two good arms.

Masters didn't even have the courage to look at him when he

said it. Which made Wyatt feel like there was something more going on.

Had the guy fucked up?

With that possibility riding his thoughts, Wyatt rose. He'd call Sanderlin tomorrow to take a look at his X-rays and MRIs. "Is this all you have for me?" Wyatt asked.

Masters' face went rigid. "I'd be happy to refill your pain medication if you still need it."

"No thanks." He'd rather feel the pain than become dependent on the meds.

There was definitely something wrong here. Masters wouldn't be so defensive otherwise, and so eager to write a prescription Wyatt hadn't used in months. "Why don't you want me talking to Dr. Sanderlin?"

"He's already gone over the findings with me."

"I'm the patient, and it's my arm."

"He's busy with his own patients."

Wyatt had the sudden urge to ram the guy's head through a wall. Every muscle in his body tensed with the need to do it. "I guess we'll find out."

He'd never given up on anything during his SEAL career. But this man of medicine was giving up. Or had fucked up. Wyatt opened the door and walked out. Masters called after him, but Wyatt ignored him and kept going.

By the time he got to the ground floor Wyatt had a plan. He could get his records digitally, but he needed copies of every X-ray and MRI he'd gotten, and the surgical notes from his procedures. He swung by the medical records department, requested a form, and took his time filling it out. If Masters was no longer willing to help him, he'd find someone who would. Even if he had to go to a civilian specialist.

Pressure built inside his chest and weighted his shoulders as he drove away from the hospital. He wasn't fit to be around anyone right now—there was too much rage burning inside him. He'd never been like this before. Even working through the pain of the initial injury hadn't made him this angry.

Once outside, he got in his car and turned it toward the training center. He needed to work off some of his anger. The parking lot was full, so he parked on the street, paid the meter, and got his gear out of the trunk.

He entered the building and breathed in the combination of sweat, cleanser, and leather that lingered in the air before striding past three boxing rings with practice bouts going on, and reached the back of the gym where exercise machines, weights, mats, and equipment were set up. Behind those were the locker rooms. He nodded to two guys he recognized as they exited the locker room while he walked past long rows of lockers until he reached his, stowed his uniform, and changed into his workout clothes.

He claimed one of the mats and took up a shoulder-width stance with his feet as he raised his right hand in the air to stretch and raised his face toward the ceiling. But his left arm still couldn't extend completely, so he had to ease into it.

And while he was at it, he needed to block out Masters' negative assessment of his prospects. If he dwelled on it, his anger might get the best of him and he could injure himself. He bent at the waist to let his injured arm pendulum toward the ground. He rocked, letting it circle clockwise, then counterclockwise, loosening up the tight muscles. He clasped his hands and raised his arms over his head, feeling a twinge, but it was still doing okay.

Bob Jarvis, the owner of the place, approached him. "How you doin', Rodeo?"

Jarvis, a retired Petty Officer, welcomed Navy personnel into the gym. Even gave them a discount on memberships, and froze their memberships when they had to deploy so they weren't out a monthly payment.

Wyatt continued to do lunges. "I'm okay." He wished it was true.

"Anything I can do for you?"

Build me a new arm. "No, I'm good. How about you?"

"I'm good. Busy." Jarvis eyed him. "Are you sure you're okay?"

He wanted to say everything he was thinking out loud just to see if he sounded crazy. But he'd been trained to keep things to himself. "I'm okay."

"If there's anything you need, just let me know."

"Thanks. I appreciate it."

Jarvis squeezed his good shoulder and went on to the next client.

Wyatt worked through the rest of the exercises the physical therapist had him do three times a day. Then moved on to the heavier routine to warm up his muscles. It helped to work up a sweat so he'd feel like he was doing something physical, even if his arm didn't always cooperate. He could position his hand if he looked at it, but the periods of numbness and of sudden pain were becoming more constant.

He would rather live in constant pain than lose the movement in his hand. That was something the doctor didn't seem to understand.

He'd find someone who would work with him on this, and he'd fight the doctor's plan to discharge him. He'd challenge it in every way he could.

When he finished his warmup, he put on his left glove and laced it one-handed, then asked one of the attendants to do the right one. He approached one of the big bags. It felt good to attack the bag. It helped him shove the emotions he refused to acknowledge back in their place.

He had no other choice. Where would he go from here? Back to Texas when his whole life was here? Fuck that!

He pounded the bag with a combination of punches. He could hit the bag with his left hand, and although he couldn't feel the contact, he could monitor the strike visually. The strength and directionality behind the blows weren't there, but every time he rocked the bag with his right punch he felt satisfaction.

After forty-five minutes, sweat ran down his face while he hammered, kneed, and kicked the bag until his muscles quivered like jelly and he was gasping for breath.

He couldn't dispute the weak performance of his left arm and hand. But if nothing else, he wanted a second opinion on the state of the nerves and whether or not there was a possibility of improvement.

Though he'd pampered it, his injured shoulder ached as he stumbled into the men's locker room and stripped down for a shower. The pain let him know he was still in the fight. The hot water eased the discomfort a minor degree, but he'd be glad to get home and ice it.

At his apartment complex, he parked his car and caught the elevator to the third floor. He tossed his gym bag into the laundry room and retrieved a beer from the fridge. Next he stuffed a bag of peas into an old T-shirt and tied it in place around his shoulder, then stretched out on the couch and closed his eyes.

He woke at a knock on his door and rolled to his feet. His shoulder felt a bit better. He untied the soggy bag of peas and shrugged it off, then looked through the peephole. Two SDPD patrol officers stood in the hall.

What the hell?

He ran through his day. Why would they be here?

One of the officers knocked on the door again. Wyatt reached for the doorknob, then hesitated. He reached for his phone on the coffee table and texted the team with "9-1-1 ASAP at home."

He turned his phone to video and opened the door. The two patrol officers were so young they looked like Boy Scouts. "Hey, officers. What's going on?"

"Are you Petty Officer Wyatt Taylor?"

"Yes."

"May we come in and talk with you for a few minutes?"

"What about?"

"We've been asked to do a wellness check on you, sir."

Wyatt laughed. He folded his arms and cocked a brow. "How do I look to you?" He glanced at the name on the man's uniform. "Officer Whitman?"

"You appear to be in pretty good physical shape, sir." He saw the man's interest in his shoulder.

"That looks like a painful injury, sir. Are you on medication for it?"

"Ibuprofen."

"Have you been experiencing any depression?" Whitman's partner asked.

"No, Officer...Norton." *Only rage.* Rage that he was keeping under careful control right now. "Who requested this wellness check?" He could guess.

"We really don't know, sir. We were just told to drive by and check on you."

"Well, you've done your job. You can make your report and say I'm sober, not depressed, not taking any medication other than Ibuprofen, and about to have company."

"May we come in and take a look around, sir?"

Wyatt studied the man's face. "Since when does a wellness check require an unauthorized search of my home?"

The two men exchanged a look. "Do you have any weapons on the premises, sir?"

"I have a registered Sig in my gun safe. It is my personal weapon and legally registered."

"May we see the registration, sir?"

He pulled his wallet out of the back pocket of his pants, removed the document, and handed it over.

While Officer Norton looked it over, the elevator opened down the hall. Teammates Stephan Kowalski and Ty Hogan stepped off the elevator and strode toward him. Both men were over six feet, broad-shouldered and in fighting shape. Their bulk dwarfed the two police officers.

"Hey, Rodeo," Kowalski studied the two police officers with narrowed hazel eyes while he extended his hand and drew Wyatt in for a shoulder bump. "Thanks for inviting us over."

"Glad you could come." Wyatt extended his hand to Ty. "Good to see you, Flirt."

"You, too."

"Go on in. I'm almost finished here. There's beer in the fridge if you want one, guys."

The officer returned his registration document.

"Everything looks in order, sir."

The elevator opened again. Mason Bishop and Eric Thorsten stepped out with Danny Wilder. Wyatt raised a hand in greeting as they strode down the hall. Thor stared at the police officers with a frown meant to be intimidating. The two officers exchanged a look.

Wyatt returned the document to his wallet and asked, "Are we good, officers?"

Norton kept his attention focused on him, "Yes, sir."

"Have a good night, and stay safe out there."

"Thanks, sir." The two walked down the hall.

Wyatt watched them get on the elevator before he went into the apartment and closed the door.

"What's going on, Rodeo?" Kowalski asked.

"I had a run-in with my doctor today and he sicced the police on me and called it a wellness check. I could see they were working their way up to making it a thing and searching my apartment."

"Looking for what?"

"They mentioned prescription drugs and weapons. I have my personal weapon in a gun safe, but I threw out the pain meds the doctor prescribed two months ago. I've been sticking with Ibuprofen. Even without the meds and without a blood test, they'd have made a case and put me on forty-eight-hour hold against my will." Something no SEAL needed on his record.

"You sure it was the doc."

"He's the only one I've had a run-in with. I asked to speak to his supervisor and he got all pissy." Masters had fucked up, and he was trying to cover his ass by attempting to ruin Wyatt's rep. It was the only thing that made sense.

"About what, Rodeo?" Kowalski asked.

He scanned the expectant faces. He'd painted himself in a corner with that one. "He wants me to accept a medical discharge."

Every man looked away. Ty's murmured, "Fuck!" held a wealth of regret and sympathy.

"I was at PT when Masters called and wanted me to stop by

his office. I hadn't seen him in nearly a month. That in itself was.... strange. Then the whole time I'm in his office he's acting nervous, avoids looking at me, blinking fast... all the telltale signs of lying. Then toward the end of the visit he got real eager to give me a new prescription for stronger pain meds. It wasn't until he insisted that I couldn't ask for a second opinion, and that I had to deal with just him, that I got pissed and walked out."

"He didn't say anything about you moving into another PCS?" Kowalski asked.

"No. He wants me gone. Offered me another six months before discharging me."

"What are you going to do?" Thor asked.

"I've already put in a request for all my medical records and the notes from the surgeries and procedures I've already undergone. If I can't get in to see the head guy, Sanderlin, I'll take everything to a civilian doctor to look over."

"If he's fucked up, you can sue him," Mason said. "Congress has rescinded the Feres Doctrine."

He hadn't thought about suing. "I just want my arm fixed." And if the guy had done permanent damage to it, Wyatt would fuck with him every way he could. Through channels and outside of them.

"You can always roll into a support position for the teams, Rodeo. You're a solid SEAL, and you'll have the backing of the entire team," Wilder said.

But with his hand still numb and his arm nowhere near full strength, they'd boot him. And even if they didn't, being on the periphery wouldn't be the same. It wouldn't be what he wanted.

Every time they deployed without him it would rip his heart out.

And moving on with his arm still fucked up.... even partially...wasn't acceptable either. The Navy was obligated to put him back together, especially since he was injured during training.

"I appreciate the backup, Thor."

He noticed a look pass between the five of them, and he suddenly felt like he was on the outside looking in.

"We'll be going wheels up tomorrow at zero five hundred, Rodeo," Kowalski said getting to his feet. "We just got word today. I was about to call you when you texted."

They were being deployed. Without him. And even though he'd known it was going to happen, it was like a stab to the gut. They'd moved on without him because they had to.

He sucked in a breath and kept his voice light and steady by sheer will. "I'm glad you were able to come by tonight, then." In his mind they were still his team, his family, his friends.

"How's Staples doing now he's released for duty?" he asked.

"He's been transferred to another platoon," Mason said, deadpan.

Wyatt nodded. "I don't hold any ill will toward him. He was falling, and it's natural to want to survive. If he hadn't latched onto me, he'd have been killed. I hope the experience will drive him toward being the best SEAL he can be."

Thor stood, offered his hand, and tugged him in for a shoulder bump. "He owes you at least that much, Wyatt. And if he doesn't take this second chance seriously, Commander Yazzie will barbeque his ass and serve it to him for breakfast."

"Good." He walked the five of them to the door. After a few more backslaps and shoulder bumps, they were gone.

The silence closed in around him. The careful control he'd maintained over his emotions all day cracked, then crumbled away. Pain and grief ripped through him like shrapnel. Tears stung his eyes. He leaned back against the door, sank to the floor, and buried his face in the crook of his one good arm.

CHAPTER 2

Eight months later

KINLEY STARED AT the computer screen. She'd put out job postings on several sites and received very little interest. What she could afford in salary was fair for the work and hours expected, but instead of qualified help, she'd gotten three college students looking for part-time work. Hoping to find someone worthwhile, she printed the applications off and leaned back in her seat to read through them.

There was a high school student who could only work on the weekends and after school. Three college students with impossible hours. She needed someone who could be here full time. Someone with experience managing a stable.

When a knock came at the door, she set the stack of papers aside with a relieved sigh and rose to answer it. A man stood outside her door, tall and broad-shouldered. She took in his arresting good looks while his attention was focused farther down the barn. His high cheekbones and prominent brow ridge spoke of some Native American heritage, but his sun-tipped light brown hair and heavy brows of the same color watered it down several generations.

"Can I help you?" Kinley asked.

He turned his head to look at her, and his tawny brown eyes seemed to have taken on the same sun-glazed hue so they matched the lighter shades in his hair. He needed a haircut, and his jaw, shadowed by dark brown scruff, was angular and sloped to a chin that could only be described as stubborn. Her attention settled on his mouth. His full bottom lip seemed too lush to be combined with such blatant masculinity. She found it sexy as hell.

"You might want to call the vet. The mare in the stall at the end is foaling."

"Oh, shit!" Kinley rushed out of the office to the farthest end of the barn. When she reached the stall, she found Tangerine moving restlessly around the enclosure, curling her top lip, shuffling her hind legs, and urinating.

She'd checked on her an hour earlier and hadn't seen any change in her behavior, but things had obviously progressed since then. Kinley whipped her phone out of her back pocket and texted Hunter, Tangerine's owner, then called the vet.

After she ended the call, she looked up from her phone to find him watching her.

Despite the situation, an instant attraction sparked a tingle in places she tried to ignore. "I'm Kinley Green. I manage the stables. Can I help you with something?" she asked.

He extended his right hand. "Wyatt Taylor." He shook her hand with just the right amount of pressure, not too hard, like he wanted to prove his manliness, and not too soft, so he wouldn't treat her like a frail female. "I saw a posting for a stable manager and decided to drop my application by on the way into town." He extended an envelope to her.

Dressed in jeans, a long-sleeved cotton shirt of pale green, and cowboy boots, he looked like any other Texan. But there was something about the way he held himself and stood that was different. He'd removed his straw hat and gripped it by the crown like a true Texan, and he'd recognized the mare was laboring, so maybe he knew his way around a horse.

Gerald Hawbecker sauntered into the barn. He eyed Wyatt with brief interest. "I just came in to check on Tangerine."

"I've already called the vet."

"She's in labor?" His brows rose and concern tightened his

features. "I'll go check on her." Gerald went to the stall door but didn't go in.

Wyatt's deep voice drew her attention back to him. "You're about to get very busy, and you have my information there."

Gerald spoke over his shoulder. "She's sweating and the placenta's presenting. I think we need the vet."

"I've already called him, and he said he'd be here as soon as possible."

"After what happened last time..." Gerald started.

Kinley cut him off. "She's going to be okay, Gerald." She couldn't think about what happened before. Tangerine was inconsolable, and had grieved for the loss of the foal, a colt, as had all the employees who helped care for the horse.

"If you'd like me to, I can stick around until the vet shows up." Wyatt said.

Her attention snapped back to him. "How much experience do you have?"

"Ten years. I worked on my dad's spread from the time I could carry a bucket. I was working on a veterinary degree to become a large animal vet when I decided to go into the Navy instead. I've been discharged for four months and I've been working with my dad's horses since I moved back. We've had four mares foal since I've been back."

"Go get the man some gloves, Gerald."

"Okay." He rushed across the barn to a door and disappeared inside.

Wyatt unbuttoned his shirt and shook free of it. Then handed it off to Kinley.

His sleeveless T-shirt molded to his chest and abdomen, outlining the sculpted musculature beneath. The red scar on his shoulder seemed obscene against the perfection of the rest of his skin. He put the obstetric glove on his left hand and arm, but it took him longer to do the right. She was moved to help him, but decided not to.

"There's one last thing you should know. Tangerine doesn't trust easily. Her owner moved her to another stable right after her colt died. She flinches away when you try to touch her, and she'll nip."

"I'll be careful."

HE COULD DO this. He might not have been around horses much since joining the Navy, but he hadn't forgotten how to care for them. In the past month he'd assisted four horses birthing their foals. One had been a tricky birth, where he ended up having to reach inside the mare and reposition a front leg and the head.

Wyatt opened the stall door and cautiously approached the mare standing in the corner. He was a stranger, and she was laboring to give birth. And now he knew she also had trust issues. He kept his voice to a hushed rumble as he said, "It's alright, Mama. I'm just here to help if you need me."

Milk dripped from her teats, and her body was covered in a fine film of sweat. Her tail had already been wrapped in preparation for the birth. As he approached, her water broke, and the placental sac protruding from the horse's vulva bulged as the shape of one hoof inside became visible.

The horse went to her knees and lay on her side. She kicked and kept raising her head to look at her stomach while she labored. He waited for the next hoof to appear. If it didn't, he'd have to reach in and get things going in the right direction.

Fifteen long, slow minutes later and still no hoof. He eased closer and stroked her contracting belly. "It's okay, Mama, I'm just going to check on that other hoof." He eased his hand inside the birth canal. Every time a contraction hit, his arm was squeezed. He felt the edge of a hoof, grabbed it, and straightened the limb. He eased inside once more to find out how the head was positioned. Now the other leg had been straightened, the head fell forward between.

He pulled his arm out. "The head will appear in a few minutes." Ten more minutes, and the foal's head shoved forward from the mare's body. This was when it was most difficult *not* to help, and time seemed to drag. When the rest of the foal's body slid free, Wyatt breathed a sigh of relief. He moved quickly to grip the placenta with his numb hand, and with his right, quickly tore it open, freeing the foal's front legs and head. The foal spontaneously took several breaths and lay on its side, recovering from the birth.

"Hey, Wyatt. How's she doing?"

Recognizing Dr. Culver's voice, he glanced up. "She's doing fine. The foal is breathing."

Even as he spoke, the mare turned to look at her baby and shifted around in the straw to lick the foal.

Wyatt peeled more of the placenta away. "It's a filly."

He stood from his crouched position and moved to the stall door. "I was just lending moral support more than anything." He peeled the wet gloves off his arms, folding them inside each other, and dropped them into a waste receptacle nearby.

Doctor Culver raised a brow at that, his eyes on the gloves. "I'm glad you were here. Her last foal was born breech and didn't make it."

"That's a shame." Wyatt was just relieved things went right this time.

Dr. Carter nodded. "I'll give her a few minutes to bond, then I'll go in and knot the placenta so she won't step on it when she gets up."

Wyatt turned his attention back to Kinley Green. Her pale eyes looked as blue as the Texas sky and her wide, expressive mouth gave him a hard-on. Or it might just be the high he got from a successful mission.

She offered him his shirt. And he turned to slide his damaged arm into the sleave first.

"Why don't you come into the office and let's talk about the job," she said.

He smiled. "Sure."

"IF YOU'D LIKE to wash up, you can use the bathroom there," she pointed to the door on the right just inside the room.

"Thanks, I will."

Once he emerged, Kinley gestured toward one of the chairs in front of her desk and took her seat. "I appreciate you stepping up to the plate like you did. I admit I've been present during numerous births, but I've never felt comfortable helping. And we've all been a little concerned about Tangerine because of what happened last time."

"No problem."

"Why do you want to work here, Mr. Taylor? You obviously have way more experience than anyone else who's applied for the job."

"After ten years, I separated from the Navy and moved back to Texas. My family lives here. Working with horses is something I'm comfortable doing and have experience with. So, it's been my fallback position since I came home."

"Why did you *separate* from the Navy?"

"I was injured during a mission, went in for surgery, and the doctor fixed my shoulder but screwed up and left the nerve in my elbow constricted. I've had two surgeries since to improve the damage, but it's left me with permanent nerve damage in my left forearm and hand." He raised the arm to elbow height and closed his hand into a loose fist. "I couldn't move into a support position, the head shed didn't want me, so the Navy cut me loose."

The words *cut me loose* didn't exactly express an amiable separation. He was partially disabled. And he'd be helping disabled children. Maybe it could be a mutually beneficial situation for him and the children. It could help him adjust to what had happened and let them see an adult who was working through some of the same challenges they faced.

But first she needed to know he had the temperament and the patience for the job.

"You know what it's like working in a stable." she said more as a statement than a question.

"Yeah. I worked on my dad's spread from the time I could

walk until graduating from high school. I came back the last two summers of college and worked for him. The work is never-ending."

"Aren't you working for him now?"

"Yeah, and I need to step away. And to be up-front with you... Dad's had some issues adjusting to the new me. I played quarterback on the football team in high school, had trophies for other sports, all the things you can do with two good arms. The reality of what's happened hasn't sunk in yet. Then on the other hand, my mom's..." He shook his head.

She couldn't help but smile. She'd seen it all before. His parents were either coddling and comforting or pressuring and pushing him to do what they thought was best, and of course making things harder for Wyatt's own adjustment. It didn't matter that he was a grown man or that he needed to find his way on his own.

"Dad wants to put me on the payroll, but he already has a full crew. In my opinion, nepotism has never done anything but cause trouble in the ranks, and I don't want to draw a salary doing a job he doesn't really need me to do."

"Are you still doing PT and therapy?"

"No. Not anymore. I do the physical therapy recommended by the PT. But I'm done with the therapist. He's signed off if you need to see my paperwork."

She supposed the military had paperwork for everything. "Most of what you'll be doing is handling the boarded horses, doing the paperwork for their care and maintenance, and keeping a record of when they're ridden. We keep strict records as proof that they're being cared for properly, as well as seeing to their grooming and hoof care. We board twenty horses, and their owners will be coming in to ride. Some come every day. We have two hands who are scheduled to feed and water in the mornings, while the other two groom and care for them. We turn the horses out for part of each day, and if an owner comes in while they're in the pasture, one of the hands has to go out and bring them in.

"For the most part, during the day we know the owner's

schedules, and most call before they arrive and we're able to rotate the horses in and out as needed. Most owners deal with their own tack, but some are on tight schedules, so we help them out if they need us to. We have a storage room for their use, and they leave their saddles and other gear here if they're daily or weekly riders."

"I have a part-time worker, Morgan Baumann, a student who comes in after his classes at the university and stays until nine for the riders who come in after six. Most of those people have their own tack and will groom and feed their horses themselves after they've ridden."

"In Stable B, we have five horses trained to work with special needs youngsters. And another group of twelve that we use for scheduled tourist rides. On occasion you may need to step in and take a group on a ride if someone's out sick, so you'll have to familiarize yourself with the trails accessible from here. If you'd like, we'll pick a Sunday and do a ride so you'll know some of the usual routes. The tourist rides have been slow so far, but the further into summer we get, the more often there'll be back-to-back rides, depending on the size of the groups.

"I'll be managing the therapy and tourist barn. And for the most part my team will do the tourist rides while I'm working with the therapy patients, but on occasion I may ask for help.

"Weekends are busy and hectic because we have so many riders who only ride then because they work during the week. If the owners ride on the weekend, they groom their own horses. I have a rotating schedule so my workers only have to work two weekends a month in pairs. You'll have two weekends off a month."

She drew a deep breath. "After everything I've said thus far, think your still game?"

"I can handle this, Ms. Green."

She nodded. "We'll have to call the farrier in to do the hoof care, and we try to schedule that a few horses at a time when we see they need it. And of course we notify the boarding owners when their mount needs attention.

"We have eight grazing pastures, and we rotate them so we don't overgraze an area. That way we know where each horse is at all times. It helps us round them up when they need to be brought in for rides. Gerald's on your team, and he knows the horses well. He'll be a big help to you.

"We also have a couple of stallions who need to be segregated because of their high-strung behavior. I'll point them out to you and show you the pasture where we usually put them."

She had to say it. "You don't think your arm will be an issue?"

"No. I've adapted, and if I feel I need help I'll ask for it."

Her throat tightened with emotion at something she saw in his expression, and she swallowed.

She decided to focus on his broad shoulders to keep her attention from wandering to that limb. When he took off his shirt during Tangerine's foaling, she noticed the slight difference in the musculature between his left arm and the other. Nerve damage or not, his shoulders, chest, upper arms and back were toned and muscular. His jeans hugged thighs just as fit.

So what if one arm was a little messed up. He was still gorgeous…which could be a problem. The female hands were going to be attracted to him like bees to a flower. Not to mention the female clients. She blocked out that thought as she continued.

"You're okay with the hours?"

"I'm used to rising early and working until dark."

"I'll have to do a background check and a drug test. It's standard practice."

"I understand. My record's clean, and I've never been arrested."

"It usually takes about a week for that to come back. After that, why don't we do a trial run for a month to make certain it's a good fit for us both." God, she wished she hadn't said it quite that way. Her face burned.

"Sounds good," Wyatt said.

There was humor in his expression, and when he smiled for the second time, she felt the punch of attraction from her midriff to the bottoms of her feet. She was probably making a huge mistake hiring him. "I'll call you tomorrow with the appointment for the drug test, and I'll push through the background check."

A knock came at the door and he stood. "Duty calls," he said. She rose to walk him out.

"You can fill out the paperwork next week so you'll be on the payroll, and then I'll show you around." And she'd see how the clients responded to him.

SHE OPENED THE door and a man stood outside, impatience in his expression, aggression in his body language. "Why didn't you call me about Tangerine, Kinley?"

Wyatt studied the man's face, and recognition hit him.

"You told me not to call, Mr. Wagner, just to text. So that's what I did." She used a calm, reasonable tone, hoping to deescalate his anger. "Tangerine is fine. She had a normal labor and birth, and she and the filly are in the stall bonding. Dr. Carter came by to make certain she passed the afterbirth without issue."

She glanced at her watch. "The filly is probably standing by now. It's been about half an hour since she was born. Let's go see."

"Stop talking to me like I'm one of your imbecile clients."

Color rose in Kinley's cheeks, but her eyes remained steady on the man's face. "Because of Tangerine's unfortunate issues last time, I thought you'd want an update on everything, Mr. Wagner. I'm sorry you find the details of the birth uninteresting. Tangerine's stall is at the end on the left. She's your horse, but it might be best if you don't enter the stall. She'll be very protective of the baby. The vet usually likes to give them twenty-four hours to bond and recover before they're disturbed. In the meantime, I have other work to do. Good afternoon." She strode away from him, her back ramrod straight as she moved in the direction opposite to where she'd pointed.

When the guy turned to face him, Wyatt continued to study him.

"What are you still standing around for, don't you have some work to do?" Wagner asked.

"Hunter Wagner?"

"Yeah. Do I know you?" The question was belligerent.

"Yeah, you should. We went to school together."

Now Wyatt was looking him in the eye, he could see Wagner hadn't changed much. He was a little heavier, his hair a little sparser, and he was still the rude, obnoxious prick he'd been since first grade. By treating him like the golden child throughout his life, his parents made certain he maintained that status all the way through school and probably through college. He was certainly exhibiting it now.

He wondered why Hunter was so aggressively obnoxious with Kinley? Had he asked her out and she'd turned him down?

"You're Wyatt Taylor. I heard you were back. Heard you got kicked out of the Navy."

Wyatt controlled the sharp jolt of anger and smiled instead. "Some things never change, do they? You haven't. Your attempts at insulting me in second grade were better than that one. Let me see if I can guess what you do for a living now." He took a step back and eyed him up and down. Expensive suit, shined shoes, white shirt, and a tie that probably cost more than his boots. "I'd say a lawyer."

"Why do you say that?"

"Suits your temperament and would make the most of your special talents," he laid in disgust in his tone.

Hunter's face tightened. "I can get you fired, Wyatt."

"No, you can't, Hunter, because I don't work here." *Not yet.*

"Oh, that's right. You always worked for your father when you weren't at college."

"I don't work there either."

That surprised him, so much that his eyebrows shot up.

Wyatt was beginning to enjoy fucking with this guy. "I take care of problems for a living. Just as I have the past ten years." That wasn't a lie. Every mission was a problem to be solved. And so was working on a ranch.

He'd dealt with plenty of dangerous situations as a SEAL. And though he didn't sense any danger from Hunter, he sensed the same animosity Hunter seemed to bear toward anyone who dared to believe they were his equal.

"Are you threatening me?" Hunter demanded.

Wyatt laughed. "Are you a problem, Hunter?"

Wyatt could almost see the wheels turning in the guy's head. If he said yes, it would be a challenge he wasn't up to, and if he said no, he'd be backing down.

Hunter settled on, "No," his tone sullen.

"I'm glad to hear it. You have a good evening." He sauntered out of the barn.

Kinley was standing at the open door to a storage area with Gerald and a woman portioning out feed and hay for the stocks' evening meal. Wyatt raised a hand as he walked by. If Hunter caused her a problem, he'd deal with him the same way he dealt with Dr. Masters.

CHAPTER 3

KINLEY FLOPPED FACEDOWN on the bed and groaned. Every muscle in her body ached. Surely this stomach flu working its way through her employees was bound to peter out soon. After hitting the beginning of the week she'd had an average of one out each day, and she'd covered for every one of them on top of her other work.

And bless Gerald for always stepping up when problems hit. For the past few days, he'd been everywhere at once when she needed him.

But the paperwork was piling up, and she needed another full-time manager—fast.

The two barns were her babies. But the ranch also belonged to her grandparents. They trusted her to succeed, and thus far she was doing well. But with success came….

It was so hard to turn over the reins.

She had to keep going for the rest of the week and then she could turn the boarders over to Wyatt.

It had been five days since he applied, and his background check came through clean. It had listed the bases where he'd been assigned, and the dates he joined and was discharged ten years later, but little else.

But he had a take-charge attitude, and while he'd been in the Navy he'd probably been in charge of things more important than horses and their riders. He'd been quick to take charge of Tangerine and adjusted the foal's position so the birth went well, thank God, and then tore away the placenta from the foal after she gave birth.

She was okay with giving meds, helping the farrier when he came to tend to their hooves, and had even broken horses and ridden in competitions, but something about sticking her hand...

He'd handled it. In fact, despite his arm injury, he looked like he could handle anything she threw at him.

Including herself.

She groaned and buried her face in the covers. Nope, she would *not* go there. Her thoughts wanted to drift to her last dating experience, and she refused to do it. Colter may have fooled her for a time, but she figured things out, and he was now out of her life—even if the embarrassment still lingered. God, how had she let him play her like that?

Wyatt had experience with horses and had worked for his father.... He had no experience being in charge of the whole thing. And she needed him to be good at running Barn A so she could relax and do what she needed to do in Barn B.

She was getting into a panic for no reason. He was going to be fine. He had a kind of presence about him that just yelled *I'm in charge*, without him having to say a word. And the women customers were going to love him. He was polite, direct, and had a wry sense of humor. She thought about his quick smile when she made the comment about him being a good fit. She bet he would be.

She groaned again, rolled onto her back and threw an arm over her eyes. She didn't want to go there.

Liar.

He'd be an employee in a few days, and strictly off limits.

The doorbell rang and she swore. *Who could that be?* She parked her golf cart around back so no one would know she was home. She forced herself to her feet. In the living room, through the window, she glimpsed a shadow move on the front porch. Reaching the front door, she looked through the peep hole and grinned. It took only a second to unlock the door.

Shelley, her best friend and co-conspirator in all things, held a pizza in one hand and a six-pack of beer in the other. "I come bearing food and drink."

Kinley watched a drop of condensation roll down one of the bottles. and shoved open the storm door. "Get in here. I could eat the north end of a southbound elephant."

Shelley laughed, sauntered into the house, and headed for the open kitchen area of the living space. She slid the pizza box onto the island counter, tucked the beer carton into the fridge, and then pulled out a bottle.

Kinley got out plates and set them on the island. Shelley wrestled the lid off the beer and shoved it into her hand. Kinley brought it to her lips and hummed in appreciation as the ice-cold brew slid down her throat. "Oh *God*, that's good."

Shelley shook her head, and her dark sable pony tail snagged over her shoulder. "Forgive me for saying this, but you look like shit, Kin." She went to a cabinet, got a glass, and got the iced tea out of the fridge.

"God it's been a hellacious day. I don't think I even got to pee today." She slid onto one of the barstools at the island and grabbed the slice of pizza Shelley put on her plate. She moaned for the fourth time since arriving home, this time in pleasure.

"You take your work much too seriously, Kin." Shelley hiked her butt up on one of the barstools. "All work and no play makes Kin a dull girl."

"I didn't really have a choice today. Two of my people were out sick with a stomach bug. I'm hoping they'll be back before the next two come down with it. Otherwise I may drop in my tracks."

"I can help fill in for a few days in the mornings before I go to work," Shelley offered.

"I've got some part-timers coming in tomorrow. Two college students who can only work about twenty hours a week. One will work mornings and the other afternoons. That will get me through until everyone gets past this bug and my new manager starts and takes over the boarding stable."

"New manager?" Shelley paused mid-drink. "You found

someone."

"Yeah. I've known for a while that I need help, but this stomach bug has driven it home. I just got his background check, and he's clean. I'll call him in a few hours and ask him if he can start right away…after I've refueled and rehydrated, thanks to you." She tipped the beer in appreciation.

Shelley's silence brought her head up. "What?"

"It's about damn time. You've nearly plowed yourself into the ground running the business. You've done the work of ten people. And besides that, I miss us doing stuff together. We haven't been four-wheeling in forever, or shopping, or any of the girl stuff we used to do on the weekends."

Guilt hit her. Shelley was right. They talked on the phone but rarely had a girls' night out for a movie, or did anything other than catch a meal together on the weekends. "Well, maybe I'll have time to do something in a couple of weeks, once he's settled into the job. It's a seven-day-a-week thing, Shelley. I have to be certain he's up for it and can handle everything."

"If you weren't sure, you wouldn't be hiring him, Kin. Throw him in the deep end of the pool and let him sink or swim."

He was in the Navy. She was certain he could swim. But…could Wyatt settle for running a stable after the action and adventure he probably experienced while on active duty? And could he do it while recovering from the injury that took all that away from him? Would she be hiring him if she wasn't so desperate?

"I need to see him in action to be certain, Shell. I have a lot of people depending on me."

"I know." Shelley rested a hand on her arm briefly. "I hope this works out."

Shelley picked up her glass to take a drink, then paused. "Forgot the most important question. What does this guy look like, and what did he do before he applied for the job?"

"He was in the Navy for ten years, but he's from here. His parents own a ranch here."

"What's his name?"

"Wyatt Taylor."

"Judge Taylor's son?" Shelley asked.

"I don't know."

"Tall, built, sun-bleached light brown hair, brown eyes that have a kind of gold tint to them."

"Yeah, that's him."

"He was a star quarterback in high school. Got a full ride to Texas A&M. But dropped out after only a year to join the military."

"How do you know all this?"

"I went to high school with him. I was three years behind him. Had a huge crush on his best friend Logan. The two were joined at the hip. And while Wyatt played quarterback, Logan played wide receiver. Those two were like brothers. They could do it all, but didn't act like spoiled, arrogant jocks. All the girls were crazy about them."

"Did Logan go into the military too?"

"No. He was killed in a car wreck the middle of his sophomore year in college. Wyatt was with him, but Logan was driving. Wyatt enlisted that summer."

The two of them looked at each other.

She hadn't gone to school with Shelley, she'd moved into her grandparent's house when, after she finished college, they offered her a managerial position helping to run the stables. She'd been lonely and working her ass off that summer. Shelley showed up after work one day with a six pack of cold beer in one hand and a bag of takeout fried chicken in the other, and invited her to come to her house for a barbeque that weekend to meet everyone in the neighborhood.

She'd been so lucky to find a friend she clicked with so quickly. They'd grown very close over the past seven years, sharing heartbreak and success, and having so much fun together... She couldn't imagine...

"Maybe having his best friend die made it too painful for him to return to college without him," Kinley said.

"Maybe so. I guess you'll eventually have an opportunity to

find out. You know how people who work closely together talk." Shelley eyed her. "Is he still good-looking?"

Kinley answered reluctantly, "Yeah. He is. He was medically discharged because of an injury to his arm, but he says he can work around it."

"Imagine all the other things he might be able to work around," Shelley said, as she slid another slice of pizza onto Kinley's plate, even though she wasn't eating any herself.

Kinley laughed. "He'll be an employee. It isn't good business to date your employees."

"But it's good for a single girl to actually date, Kin. And I know for a fact it's been four months since you've gone out. You can't possibly be pining for that…"

"No. Not pining. I didn't really pine for him for even a day once I figured things out. But I'm still pissed." And her ego was still bruised. "But I certainly wouldn't kick Liam Hemsworth out of bed for eating crackers."

Shelley shot her a look. "As I recall, Wyatt could give Liam and Chris a run for their money."

He could, despite an injured arm. She changed the subject. "How's Landon?"

With a sigh Shelley let her get away with the change of subject and said, "He's working his ass off. He's hoping they'll promote him to manager soon, now Mark and Terry are moving to San Antonio."

"He's worked at J & G Building Supply since he was in high school, has a business degree, he's had all the managerial training, and he's been loyal to them for years. He deserves to run the show," Kinley said in support.

"But it's up to the corporate office to make the decision, and they always seem to want to ship in someone. That's how Mark and Terry got here."

"Has he asked Mark for a letter of recommendation?"

Shelley nodded, "Signed, sealed, and delivered. We're really going to need that promotion since we'll soon have another mouth to feed."

In mid-chew, it took Kinley one second, then another, for her to realize what Shelley meant. "Oh my God! Oh my God!" Emotion hit her and she had to blink away tears before she slid off the stool and wrapped her arms around Shelley.

"Don't you dare cry," Shelley warned, returning the embrace. "You'll get me started."

After a year and a half of tests, treatments, and a roller-coaster ride of hope and heartbreak, it had finally happened for them. Tears streamed down Kinley's face. She reached for a napkin to mop at them, but it was useless. The tears just kept coming. "When did you find out?"

"I've been sitting on it for four weeks, because I was afraid to believe in it. But I took a pregnancy test this morning, and it came up positive. I called the doctor's office, and they did another this afternoon. So it's official. But we're not going to tell anyone until I'm at least three months along. Only you, Kin. And if you don't stop crying, I'm going to have a meltdown myself."

"I'm trying. It's just not working. Oh, my God, you need to stay away from me." She took two big steps away. "People at work have been coming down with a stomach bug. If I gave it to you, I'd die."

"You don't feel sick, do you?" Shelley asked.

"No. I've been staying away from everyone and washing my hands every time I touch anything. And I've put out germicide everywhere. I even sprayed down the stall latches this evening. I've been spraying down the bathroom every morning and night too."

"It's been going around at work too, and I've been being careful there. I'll parboil myself when I get home," Shelley said with a grin.

Kinley laughed. "I'm so happy for you."

"I know you are. Landon wants to wrap me in cotton wool, but I know that won't work. What will happen, will happen. But I'm hopeful this time, Kin." Her voice dropped to just above a whisper, as though she didn't want the baby to hear. "If it doesn't work out, we're going to try for adoption. Even with everyone pitching in, the fertility treatments are so expensive. So that extra money will come in handy for that, too."

"It's going to be okay, Shelley. I know it will." Kinley wanted to hug her again, but was afraid to. "You need to have a pregnancy party once you've decided to tell everyone. I can host it here if you'd like. My backyard and deck are available."

"I'd love that. I'll mention it to Landon when I get home." She slid off the stool. "We'll plot and plan later. I've got food in the car for us to celebrate with tonight. But I had to bring you pizza and the news first."

Kinley started to tear up again. "I should have known when you brought it in and didn't eat you had something important to tell me." That's what they always did for each other.

She followed Shelley to the door. "I'm here for you if you need me for anything."

"I know. Always." Shelley grinned though tears shone in her eyes. "I'm going to be a mama, Kinley."

"And I'm going to be an honorary aunt."

"Honorary, hell." Shelley pointed at her. "Full-fledged godmother."

Kinley patted her chest over her heart.

After Shelley was gone, Kinley packed away the pizza, finished the beer she'd nursed, and climbed in the shower to let the warm water cascade over her tired body and help her settle down again for the night. She caught herself every time she thought of Shelley while she dried her hair and pulled on boxers and a long T-shirt.

Her home phone rang, but the number that popped up on the remote phone only said "private." Thinking it might be a client, she answered.

"Bitch—" That one word whispered into the phone was like a slap. Her heart raced, and she gripped the receiver hard. Empty silence followed, so she hit the off button and set the phone back in its cradle.

"Damn you, asshole." With that one word the person on the other end had succeeded in diminishing her pleasure.

Whoever it was spoke only in a whisper, and she wasn't able

to tell if it was a man or a woman, but there was only one person angry enough with her to do this kind of call, and she wasn't going to give him the satisfaction of calling him back. That would be exactly what he wanted.

"Screw him," she muttered to herself as she climbed into bed and turned on the television.

CHAPTER 4

WYATT DROPPED HIS car keys in a basket on the table just inside the door. The small entrance foyer opened up into a wide living room and kitchen. The high ceilings crossed by wooden beams made the space seem more expansive than it was.

The upgrades his parents did after he and his brothers took turns using the cabin as their summer residence between college classes had certainly improved the look of the place, and managed to successfully stomp out the woodsy man-cave feel he and his brothers had enjoyed.

He wouldn't dream of throwing his underwear on his bedroom floor or leaving dirty dishes in the sink for days as they'd done when younger. Partially because he'd developed more discipline since his teen years, but also because the cabin wasn't really a cabin anymore. It was a home.

He sauntered through the living room and into the kitchen, set the Asian food he'd picked up on the kitchen table, got a beer from the refrigerator, and grabbed a plate and fork.

He settled at the table, opened the cartons, and filled his plate. The doorbell rang before he was a quarter of the way through his meal. He sighed and went to the door to answer it.

His mother stood on the porch with a bag of food. "Hey, Mom."

"I went by the grocery, and while I was there, I picked up

some of your favorites." She walked past him into the kitchen and started unloading apples and bananas and putting them into a bowl. He liked fruit well enough, but he couldn't remember stating a preference for either. In fact, he liked pineapple and grapes the best. She took out carrots, celery and squash and put them in the crisper. He bought vegetables, mostly frozen because they required less work to cook. What grown man ate celery? None, if they could avoid it.

Wyatt stifled his irritation and just watched. His mom had aged well. Her light brown hair streaked with blond, so similar as his own, had only a few strands of gray that blended in so well they were close to unnoticeable. Her green eyes were sharp and missed nothing. She'd gained a little weight over the years and appeared rounder through the hips, but it only made her look more like a mom.

"Would you like some Chinese, Mom?"

"No, I have dinner in the crockpot cooking right now. I was going to invite you. We're having beef stew and cornbread." She'd been making excuses to come by every day, and she appeared so quickly after he arrived, he wondered if she was using binoculars to find out when he got home?

"I'm good."

"You didn't go in to work at the stables this morning."

Had she called the office there to check up on him, or worse, gone by? Wyatt crossed his arms and leaned back against the cabinets directly across from her, and took shallow breaths to keep his anger in check. "Is working at the stables a prerequisite to me living here?"

"No, of course not. It's just that…you usually worked there every day when you lived here before."

"About a week ago I interviewed for a job off the ranch, Mom."

She straightened and turned to face him. "Why?" She shut the refrigerator door.

Wyatt bit back the quick words on the tip of his tongue. "I want to make a living independently, not be supported by my parents."

"We're not supporting you, Wyatt."

"I'm living here rent-free, Mom." And refusing the salary his father offered him.

"So did your brothers the whole time they were home from college each summer."

"I'm not home from college, Mom."

"You could be, Wyatt. You could go back and finish your veterinarian degree."

He might decide to do that, but at the moment he was still looking at his options. "Mom, I've only been here a few of months. I need time to decide what I want to do."

The measured patience of his tone finally got through. Her expression shifted and color flushed her cheeks. "I'm not trying to tell you what to do."

Yes, she was. He tried for a gentle but firm tone. "I need some time and space, Mom. When I decide what I'm going to do I'll let you know."

He could almost see the struggle behind her carefully neutral expression. "I love you, Wyatt."

"And I love you. But think of it this way…if I'd come home with a woman, you'd have really put a crimp in my love life. It isn't a good look for a soon to be thirty-year-old man to have his mother delivering groceries. Not impressive at all."

She bit her lip then smiled. "Point taken. Have you met someone?"

Kinley Green came to mind, as she had every day for past week, but he wasn't going there. He wasn't ready for any kind of entanglement. "No. Well, maybe. I think I need to get my own situation settled before I take on any emotional baggage."

"Wyatt… Just a suggestion. If any woman discovers you look at her as emotional baggage, you'll never stand a chance. And rightfully so."

He grinned, then chuckled. "Point taken. I'll keep that in mind."

She crossed to him and gave him a hug. "I just worry about

you."

"I know." He squeezed her gently with his good arm. "And I appreciate it. But I'm not the college kid who left ten years ago."

"I know." With a sigh she pulled away. "I'll save you some stew for lunch tomorrow. You can come up to the house and pick it up."

He shook his head. She was incorrigible. "Thanks, I appreciate it."

After she left, he settled down to finish his meal. But the longer he dwelled on her eagerness to pamper him, the more his frustration level rose. A grown man running home to his parents... Just the idea left a sour taste in his mouth. And the way they looked at him, with a combination of pity and worry, was even worse.

He needed to move off the ranch and away from them, but in order to do that he needed a job. He refused to live off his disability pay. To do so was admitting defeat. He could work and make his own way. He still had one good, working arm, and the rest of him was fine.

He shoved aside the food and went over to get his laptop from the small office area he set up in one corner of the living room. Even though he'd applied for the stable job, he needed to keep looking for something more...in tune with his training.

He opened the browser and did a check on Masters. Discharged from the military, he'd settled in Florida. He'd joined a practice there and moved on with his life despite being declared responsible for doing more harm than good with Wyatt's case. It wasn't Masters' incompetence that caused his discharge, it was his attempt to lie his way out of it.

Wyatt rubbed his forehead. He wanted to get past the bitterness and move on, but the man cost him his career and left him without the full use of his left arm and hand. He hoped paying with a premature discharge from the Navy made Masters more vigilant and caring of his patients. And he hoped the money Masters would have to pay him one day would hurt worse. If the suit was ever settled.

It probably wouldn't be, though. Masters had been arrogant and unrepentant throughout the court martial proceedings. He'd probably never change.

How many other patients had he harmed? Did the Navy attempt to find out, or did they sweep it all under the rug to avoid the shit show that would have followed?

His own separation from the Navy had cut his access to everyone who might have told him anything. So he'd never know. And maybe that was what was eating at him. He needed to leave all this behind, but it still felt like things were left unfinished.

He changed his online search to college classes offered through one of the local universities. He might be able to transfer the college credits he earned after enlisting. He was halfway to finishing an IT degree. But his hand issue had nipped that in the bud.

Fifteen minutes later someone knocked on the door. He closed the laptop and rose. Judge Bryan Taylor, his father, stood on the porch wearing a pale gray business suit with his thick, salt and pepper hair brushed back from his high forehead.

When Wyatt was younger he and his father had been close. He wondered why it was so difficult to get that back. Possibly because he felt like his parents were sitting in judgment about everything he did. And his father never forgave him for dropping out of college and enlisting. "Hey, Dad."

"I need to ask a favor."

"Sure."

"We're having trouble with someone cutting our fences in the west pasture. Some of our cattle wandered out and almost got hit by a truck. I'd like you to check the fences and see that they're repaired."

"Sure. How often is this happening?"

"In the past month they've been cut four times."

"Has it been in the same area or random?"

"It's been in the same area, but in random segments. You'll need to talk to Randall about it."

Randall could handle this. He was the ranch manager, and his dad was going to cause a rift between them if he continued to push Wyatt in the foreman's way.

Getting a job off the spread was the right thing to do. "I'll talk to Randall tomorrow."

"Good."

"You want to come in, Dad?"

"No. I'm going up to the house and eat some of your mother's stew. It's been a long day. You want to come?"

"I've already eaten."

"Okay." He started to say something more, then nodded. "Your brothers will be here in a month or so for a visit. They haven't seen you since you got home, and they want to visit. You don't have anything planned on, say, the 27th, do you?"

"No, I don't have anything planned." He thought of Kinley mentioning a trail ride one Sunday. But she hadn't called about the job yet.

"We'll have a barbecue. You three can man the grill."

His father was trying too hard. "That sounds good, Dad."

"Wyatt...." His father took a step over the threshold. "Sooner or later that iron control is going to break, and I'm afraid of what might happen."

He stuffed his hands in his pockets to keep from fisting them. He wasn't going to say he was okay. But he wasn't going to snap and go crazy either. But at this moment he really, really wanted to punch something. "I really appreciate the vote of confidence, Dad." He met his father's gaze with narrowed eyes. "I don't have PTSD, and I'm not depressed. What I am is pissed that the man who ruined my career is practicing medicine and possibly damaging other peoples' lives. And that the Navy took the dickless way out and discharged him but didn't have the balls to take his license."

"How long have you known all that?"

"A month or so."

"You have to let this go, Wyatt."

"Why?"

"Because it's not healthy."

"No, it's not. Not for anyone that asshole performs surgery on."

His father shook his head. "You need to move on, Wyatt."

He didn't really have a choice about that. He couldn't just sit on his ass from now on. "I am moving on, but I'll never forget or forgive."

"They gave him a less than honorable discharge. He'll never draw his military benefits. Yes, he's practicing medicine, but he's being supervised for up to a year."

"How do you know?"

"I have my ways. He does anything underhanded again, he'll lose his license."

Wyatt studied his father's expression. "You're not just telling me that to appease me."

His father's lips thinned and he shook his head. "What makes you think I'd lie to you, Wyatt?"

"I know you wouldn't lie, but you might try to spin it so I'll stop dwelling on it."

"I'm not *spinning* anything." The terse reply held some heat.

Wyatt ignored his father's anger. "I hope whoever supervises him stays on his ass." As closely as the fucker had stalked him.

A tense silence fell between them until Bryan broke it. "How are you moving on, Wyatt?"

"I applied for a job about a week ago, and once my drug test and background check come back, I'll be working."

"You have a job here, son."

"Dad…I appreciate it. But right now, I end up stomping on Randall's toes every time you come to me with an issue. I think I can find out who's cutting your fences, but I think Randall and I should work together and make them pay to repair them when I catch them."

"And how do you expect to catch them?"

"With motion-activated cameras and a drone. They're in storage right now, but I'll get them out tomorrow. I can set alarms on my computer and phone to alert me when they come onto your property again and cut the fence. And I'll use the drone, which has

GPS, to penpoint their location. I could film them, too, but filming with a drone…"

"It's an invasion of privacy," Bryan finished for him. "Unless they're breaking the law and it's part of our security system."

"I guess we'll just have to make the drone part of your security system, at least temporarily. The security cameras can take video and still photos, though. There's no law against that. Then we'll take the evidence to the police."

"Are those some of the skills you cultivated as a SEAL?"

"Yeah. Some of it. I installed security cameras at my apartment during the investigation." To prove Masters' harassment through the use of the police. They'd shown up at his door almost weekly. "The Navy uses armed drones defensively and unarmed for intelligence gathering. I flew both kinds during missions." Would the weakness in his left hand affect his ability to fly the drone? Surely muscle memory would kick in and he'd be able to do it. He'd get the drone out so he could practice and make whatever adjustments he needed so he could fly the thing. One more adjustment, one more adaptation he had to make to maintain a skill that had come as second nature to him. He was sick of it.

He looked up to see his father watching him. "Some of us purchased personal drones and practiced our skills in the hills and desert. It was a hobby and practice for combat at the same time. I'd sometimes use mine to film wildlife. I got some pretty nice footage of whales and dolphins." And the beach bunnies. Damn, he missed California. Maybe he could move closer to the coast. Maybe Corpus Christi or Galveston.

He raked his hair back from his forehead.

"Whatever you can do, I'll appreciate it," Bryan said.

"Okay. Dad. I'll talk to Randall tomorrow."

"Thanks." Bryan strode down the porch steps but turned back. "You're sure you won't come up and have some stew? I think your mom picked up an apple pie from the Pie Company and we have some vanilla ice cream to go on it."

The harder he pulled away, the harder they clung. He swung

between guilt and resentment because of it. He wanted to be alone. Needed to be alone until... "How's half an hour? I'll come up and have a piece of pie."

"Good. I'll tell your mom."

Wyatt closed the door, raked his fingers through the hair at his temples and pressed his palms against them. He'd swallow his resentment and go just to ease their worry.

He only needed to stick it out a few more days, and he'd have a job elsewhere, somewhere his mother wouldn't be able to keep a daily eye on his movements. He'd look for an apartment off the ranch.

He could hardly wait.

CHAPTER 5

KINLEY PULLED HER heavy mass of damp hair into a ponytail and secured it with a scrunchie. She patted moisturizer on her face and added a light makeup with sunscreen. She'd learned her fair skin burned easily and tried to protect it as much as possible. A quick application of lip gloss and she was ready for the day.

She grabbed her lunch and a thermos of tea from the kitchen and left her house. As she drove to the stables, her mind raced through the schedule for the day. She sometimes wondered if all the work she did was worth it. Boarding other people's horses, giving riding lessons, leading trail rides for tourists, and working with disabled children were a lot for one stable to handle.

Her grant had only been approved for ten clients, and the paperwork she had to submit was insane, but she could already see a positive change in a few of the kids. Of the two they had scheduled for today, Joshua Mueller's behavior was improving and Katie Weber was gaining confidence when she mounted Socks and rode him. The sixteen-year-old girl was a sweetheart, but very aware that her appearance and speech were different because she had Downs Syndrome. And she was being bullied at school since she was an easy target.

At least when she was doing the therapy exercises with the horses, riding or caring for them, she could leave all that behind. And Diane, Katie's therapist, was working with Katie, her parents, and her teacher to try and solve the issue.

Kinley was certain that part of Katie's problem was her lousy relationship with her father. He treated her like a two-year-old, when in fact she picked up on things more quickly than he gave her credit for, and her speech issue was deceptive. She functioned on a seven-year-old level. With continued encouragement she'd be able to live a productive life. Maybe work at a grocery store stocking shelves or doing landscaping. She certainly loved planting flowers around Kinley's house. Also, the high school had a greenhouse, and Katie worked in it as part of her life skills class. There had to be a way to get her father to recognize her accomplishments.

Maybe she and Diane could collaborate to demonstrate Katie's progress and explain to him how it could lead to a more fulfilling life for her later if she was encouraged to continue being independent and work on her communication skills. And show her father how giving her responsibility helped her become more independent.

Kinley climbed in the golf cart parked outside the house and drove across the pastures to the gate a half mile down the road. She got out and opened the gate, drove through, then got out to close and lock it behind her.

She spotted Wyatt's black SUV already in the parking lot. The sun was barely up, backlighting his tall, muscular physique. She took in his long, muscular body as he leaned back against the hood of the vehicle and his even longer legs as he bent his knee and rested his bootheel on the bumper. A nervous jitter hit her system.

She'd gone back over his background check before calling him to come in today. It was sparse since he'd spent most of the last ten years in the Navy, and the Navy only reported on the bases he'd been assigned to, his rank at the time of discharge, and that he had no criminal record. It hadn't satisfied her curiosity at all.

As she climbed out of the golf cart, Wyatt took a final drink out of his thermos cup, emptied the last of the contents on the ground, screwed the cup back onto container, and set it in the

SUV.

She glanced at her watch as she got out of the car. He was right on time. And he looked damn good early in the morning. Handsome, well built, his amber-tinted brown eyes piercing and clear. She tried to ignore the physical response she experienced as she approached him. "The door isn't locked. It's on an automatic release at six."

"I was just finishing my coffee and checking out your spread. You've got a pretty place here."

"Thanks. The land belongs to my grandparents. They've been horse people their whole lives. My grandfather bred and sold horses and my grandmother boarded them. When they passed the torch to me, I built another barn. That's when we started giving riding lessons and trail rides. Then I applied for a grant to do the equine therapy with the disabled and got it. We have ten therapy clients."

He narrowed his gaze against the early morning sun growing stronger over the horizon. "Is that your house in the distance?"

"My grandparents'. They wanted me to live in it and take care of it. They live in Florida now, but come back for a month at Christmas and a couple of weeks in the summer."

"I understand the draw of living close to the ocean. I surfed, fished, and did deep dives in the Pacific."

"Do you miss it?"

He had a faraway gleam in his eyes. "Yeah."

Another thing he'd lost.

"But I don't miss the traffic to and from work." He shrugged. "To and from everywhere."

"My grandfather has taken up fishing since he moved to Florida. He rarely had time while he was running the stables. But we have a pretty creek that runs through the property, with some decent-sized trout, and a pond out in the west pasture that's also stocked." She gathered her lunch. "Come on in and I'll give you the paperwork to set you for payroll."

"Okay."

He got the door for her and followed her down the wide center aisle. "Did you update the roof when you took over here?" he asked.

"Yes, and the ventilation when I had the other barn built. I hired an engineer to design the best system to keep the dust down to keep the horses healthy. It also keeps the moisture in the air down so the feed and hay we store here stays mold free."

She turned into the office. His office now. She set her bag on the desk, she went to one of the filing cabinets to pull out the forms.

"Fill these out by end of business today, and I'll pass them on to Britney. She keeps the books."

She reached for a manila folder and withdrew a copy of the procedures they followed to maintain a paper trail on the care and riding of the horses they boarded.

"Each horse has its picture on the stall. They're fed twice a day. I have their weight charted, as well as the amount of feed and hay they need each time. All of them spend part of the day out in one of the pastures until they're brought in around six for their last feeding."

"Also, the horses used for trail rides are groomed by the people who ride them. Part of the experience here at Silver Cloud Stables is training the riders how to care for the animals, and by doing that the riders pay homage to them for the entertainment. The therapy horses are groomed by the clients as well."

"Why Silver Cloud?" he asked.

"The stables are named after my first horse. I started riding her when I was five. She was a paint, with a white mane and tail, and a dream to ride. I moved her here with me from San Antonio. She died last year."

"I'm sorry,"

She nodded. "Thanks." She was still more emotional about it than she wanted to let on. Sometimes maintaining a professional demeanor sucked. "It took me six months... before I decided to get another horse. So now I have Indira. She's the buckskin quarter horse in the stall next to Tangerine. She was a rescue, and had a hard time of it before coming to us. She and I are getting to know each other."

"You'll find your rhythm together," he commented.

"I'm sure we will." She thought if she asked him while they were getting to know one another.... "What did you say to Hunter Wagner the other night?"

Wyatt's gaze sharpened. "We were just catching up. I haven't seen him since high school."

"I think it was a little more than catching up. He was a different guy when he left."

Wyatt shrugged. "He wanted to know what I do for a living. I told him I'm in the business of solving problems and asked him if he was one."

Wow. "What did he say?"

Wyatt's smiled. "He said he'd get me fired for threatening him. I told him I didn't work here. Which I didn't...at the time. It threw him off, but he's much too full of it to stay cowed for long. It tripped him up for a few moments, though, and made him think."

She was relieved by the fact that he wasn't afraid to poke the bear or to deal with the consequences for doing it. "What did you do in the Navy, Wyatt?"

After a brief pause, he said, "I was a SEAL."

She knew about SEALs. Anyone with a television or a computer knew about them and what they did. "How long were you a SEAL?"

"In the Navy, ten. Eight years as a SEAL. I put in for it when I enlisted and got it."

He was one of the Naval elite. She'd watched a documentary on what a candidate endured to become a SEAL and how much training they worked through. After succeeding in all of that, it was all taken away from him by an injury. Tears burned her eyes, and she looked away. "I'm sorry for what you've lost."

"Thanks. I'd appreciate it if you keep all that to yourself. I don't really talk about it. People sometimes react strangely once they find out."

"Okay." She picked up the schedule and a marker board

marker. "I'll lay out the schedule while you do your paperwork. By the time you finish, the others will be here, and I'll introduce you before we all start work."

Gerald arrived while she was writing out the schedule. "So he took the job?" he asked.

"Yes. He's the most qualified candidate to apply. And he knows horses." She turned to look over her shoulder. "Why didn't you want the job? It would have been an increase in pay for you."

"Everyone knows me too well. They'd have taken advantage. Since he's unknown. they won't question his orders. And besides, he'll have to work his ass off nonstop, just like you do."

She laughed. "Yeah, that's true."

"I'll start the morning feedings," he said.

"Hold off on that, Gerald. I'd like to introduce him to the crew first, then show him around."

"Okay."

By the time she was halfway through the schedule, Wyatt came out of the office and eyed the board.

Several other employees arrived while she finished up. There were eight hands. She and Wyatt made ten. That made a manager for each section. Wyatt would share four hands to feed and groom and clean the stalls of the 20 horses they boarded.

And she'd be able to concentrate on the equine therapy patients, riding lessons and trail riding horses more easily.

While they were all standing at the board, she introduced Wyatt. "This is Wyatt Taylor. He'll be Silver Lining's new boarding barn manager."

She went down the line and introduced each member of the team.

Wyatt nodded to each one. "I'm glad to be here and am looking forward to working with all of you," he said briefly.

"Gerald, you and the teams can get the morning feeding going while I show Wyatt around the stables."

"Will do." He used two fingers to salute her.

She waited for a few minutes while Wyatt went to each worker and shook their hand. Then the group scattered to go to work.

"I thought I'd go down and check on Tangerine and her foal before I go to the other stable to work. I have the hands divided into teams, and they rotate feeding duties. Two take care of it in the morning and the other two in the afternoon."

Mother and baby were settled in together, and the filly was nursing. Healthy, happy mom and baby were exactly what she'd hoped for. What all the staff had hoped for, too. This one event had lifted pressure off all their shoulders.

She rested her arm on the top of the stall. When she spoke softly to her, Tangerine wandered over, but jerked away when she raised a hand to stroke her neck. When she offered Tangerine a peppermint candy she approached again, very cautiously, and finally took it.

"Her behavior has changed since we had her before. She's developed some trust issues. And she's been nipping, which she never did before." She looked up at Wyatt. "Any suggestions for how to change that."

"Where was she stabled before?"

"After she lost the foal, Wagner moved her to Myers'."

"I know Keith. Just saw him recently. He's really good with the horses. I'll call him and ask him about how she was while she was there."

"I appreciate it. I wouldn't be concerned if it wasn't such a drastic change from before. But she's doing well with the filly."

"After she has a few more weeks with her foal, I'll work with her and see if I can build some trust. Any other problems you want me to address?"

His smile set off a flutter of awareness she tried to ignore. He was an employee and she couldn't step over the line.

"No," she said. Then cleared her throat. "The other horses are doing well. The farrier will be here to tend to four horses' feet this week. I'll send you the schedule. Right now I'll show you the supply room where we store the meds and feed, and the tack room, then go over the computer programs we use. The office here will be yours from now on. I have my own in the other barn. We're networked between the two. I have a list of supply companies for feed and hay. When we need to order, we'll combine them."

"Okay."

"I'm micro-managing, aren't I?"

"Just a little." He scanned the barn, the people. "I can see how much you've put into this stable and the other. I won't let anything happen to this one. You can trust me to take care of it. If I run into trouble, I'll come find you. Remember I'm a problem-solver."

And a Navy SEAL. How could he ever settle for running a stable after that?

Had she made a mistake?

They had a month to find out. She forced a smile and took a deep breath "Okay."

CHAPTER 6

WYATT TOOK THE first couple of hours to observe and to walk every inch of the barn.

He introduced himself to each horse, checked each stall's condition and watched the hands work. He admired Kinley's system of organization and division of labor. While two hands fed the stock, the other two were busy cleaning the stalls and giving meds to those few who had issues. On the outside of each stall was a clipboard assigned to each horse. When the stall was cleaned, it was checked off. When meds were given, they were recorded.

There was running water piped through self-draining hoses from a frost-free hydrant system so watering wasn't an issue. The plastic troughs were cleaned each week, refilled each morning and the water levels checked at the end of the day. He wondered who had designed the system. It was something his dad might be interested in. And he'd need to find out if there was an issue with the water freezing in the winter. He'd ask Kinley.

The roof vents were open and the fans going, circulating the smell of hay, horses, and the pine shavings they used for bedding in the stalls. He found those scents relaxing, and being around the horses was calming as well.

After helping turn out the horses to graze that weren't scheduled to be ridden this morning, he slipped into the office to make a phone call to Keith Myers. When Keith answered, Wyatt identified himself.

"How you doing, Wyatt?" Keith asked.

"I'm good. I've taken a management position at Silver Lining stables, taking care of the boarding stables while Kinley is concentrating on the trail rides and therapy horses."

"I didn't know Kinley was looking for a manager. I'm glad you've been hired there."

"Thanks, I appreciate it."

"What can I do for you Wyatt?"

"I know you had Hunter Wagner's mare Tangerine at your place for a while."

"Yeah. She's a beauty. In my opinion he should never have moved Tangerine away from Kinley's. She received wonderful care there, and the move only stressed her more after the loss of the colt. She called for the foal for several days, and was made even more miserable because she was still lactating. It took a few weeks for her milk to dry up."

"How was her behavior toward you afterward?"

"She was anxious and restless. A few weeks later she had a strange injury to her jaw, like she might have reared back and struck it on the mount feeder in her stall. She healed quickly, and since she never had an issue eating, we just watched her closely until it healed."

"Kinley mentioned that her behavior has changed. She's a little skittish when people attempt to pet her. And she's prone to nipping. Did you observe any of that?"

"Yeah, it started in the first three months we had her. We just marked it up to the change in environment and the loss of her foal. She seemed to settle down after she was bred again. If she's started back up, maybe the move triggered it."

"I'm going to try to work with her and modify the behavior. Any suggestions?"

"Just positive reinforcement and redirection. We never really use any kind of punishment for behavior issues with the horses."

"I agree. Kindness and patience are the tried-and-true methods at my dad's place too."

"Does he still have that gelding you trained to do tricks?" Keith asked.

"Smoke? Yeah, he does. When I came home for visits, I rode him and worked with him, and I've been riding him almost daily since I've been back. He still remembers the tricks."

He'd missed the horse as much as he'd missed his family when he left for college and then the Navy. Plus, riding Smoke recently had been therapeutic for him. It gave him an understanding of what Kinley was trying to accomplish with her horses.

"If you can get a horse to dance, pick pockets and take bows, getting one to stop nipping should be a piece of cake."

"I hope so. Got to impress the boss so she'll keep me on."

"I'm going to be nosy and ask why you left your dad's spread."

"I'm not needed at the ranch. Dad has a good crew, and everything runs like a well-oiled machine. I didn't want be a disruption there." And sometimes being the boss's son caused friction. "After ten years of being away, I decided it was better for me to look for work off the ranch."

"Makes sense to me. If you need anything else, don't hesitate to call or come by."

"Thanks, I appreciate it."

He mulled over Keith's mention of Tangerine's jaw injury. It must have been pretty bad for Keith to still sound concerned about it. But then when you were responsible for someone else's property and it was damaged...

Horses weren't property to Wyatt. They had personality, showed affection, and were intelligent. But he'd bet his best boots that Hunter Wagner thought of Tangerine as property. He'd look at her and the filly as investments.

What was the point of even having a horse if you don't ride?

Wyatt pushed the old angst away. It was in the past. He needed to take some time and build a rapport with Tangerine, which was going to be difficult since she had the baby in tow. But not impossible. If there was a pattern to her behavior, it would be easier to catch on camera than through personal observation since he couldn't spend hours watching her and get his job done.

He left the office, met two clients who were there to ride, and signed them in. One went into the tack room, got her saddle and gear, and was ready to ride in a few minutes. The other, Margo Lester, was more demanding. He tacked up her mount, and was aware of her watching him as he tightened the cinch. Instead of giving her a boost into the saddle as he would have in the past, he shoved over a mounting block. Once she was in the saddle, he handed her the reins.

"Have you hurt your arm?" she asked.

Wyatt chose his words carefully. "It's a permanent condition."

"You could have instructed one of the others to saddle my mount."

"There was no need. I can do the work." Had she wanted him to lift her into the saddle? If this princess couldn't mount a horse on her own, she had no business riding alone.

"I'd like one of the others to check the cinch and make sure it's tight enough."

Wyatt gestured to Carol Poynter, one of the hands he met that morning. Carol was quick to come over. "Ms. Lester would like you to check the cinch and make certain it's tight enough."

Carol quickly checked it. "It's perfect Ms. Lester."

"It had better be." The woman looked down her nose at them both, gave a nod, and rode out without so much as a thank-you.

"I'll take care of her when she comes back, Mr. Taylor," Carol said, her lips compressed. The expression didn't suit her round, pleasant face. And her willingness to protect him said a lot about her character.

Wyatt smiled. "Thanks, Carol, but I think I need to be the one to do it." Because Margo Lester didn't want him to. And he'd prove to her that he wasn't going to take her shit.

Carol glanced up and seemed to be taking his measure. She smiled and gave a nod. "Good for you, Mr. Taylor."

Gerald wandered up after Carol had returned to grooming one of the horses. "Margo Lester is one of our two 'entitled' clients."

Wyatt raised a brow. "Is that what you call it? Are you going to give me the other one's name so I'll be warned?"

"Why should I? No one warned us."

Wyatt laughed.

Gerald relented. "The other one is Suzanne Heinz. She's only slightly less...difficult...than Ms. Lester."

"I'll make it a point to deal with her too." A thought came to him. "Do we have any kind of camera system here?"

"Hoping to catch her in the act and post it to social media?" Gerald asked.

Wyatt chuckled. "Lucky for them, I don't have any kind of social media account."

Gerald nodded. "Wise man. We have two outside cameras that cover the front door and two to cover the parking lot. Two at the back door too, but none inside."

"Just wondering."

"We've never had an issue with stealing or misconduct."

"I wasn't concerned about theft. Kinley mentioned a concern about one of the horses, and I've decided to monitor her behavior for a few days. I may be able to figure out what's triggering her."

Gerald gave him a thoughtful look. "Too bad we don't have a system."

Wyatt nodded. And his was tied up on his dad's property, monitoring the property line. Maybe after he caught the assholes who kept cutting the fences, he could mount one camera in Tangerine's stall. But so far the assholes hadn't returned.

A client came in through the open double doors and Gerald excused himself to approach her. "Hey, Ms. Dixon. It's good to see you. I think Lexi's been watching for you. She knows you're coming when she isn't turned out with the others. She'll be thrilled you're here."

"I'll be thrilled to see her, too."

Since Gerald and the others were occupied, Wyatt wandered down toward Tangerine's stall to check out the horses housed on either side of her. Kinley's Buckskin, Indira, was on one side.

Indira wandered to the stall door and poked her head out to be loved on. Wyatt offered her a peppermint and she lipped it up. On the other side was Lester, an Appaloosa with the spotted markings of the breed. He'd already been turned out into the pasture. When Wyatt stopped at Tangerine's stall, she eyed him distrustfully and stayed in the corner with the filly.

Most horses were curious and interested in everything going on around them. Tangerine seemed more watchful and defensive. Something had happened to the mare in the past year that changed her behavior. "Tell me your secrets, Tangerine, and I'll try to help," Wyatt said softly.

Two more riders came in, and he left the stall to introduce himself and lend a hand.

He checked the schedule for other riders, and seeing only two, decided that Gerald and Carol Pointer, one of the hands he met that morning, could handle things.

He settled behind his desk with some of his mother's stew and opened some of the software Kinley had mentioned.

By end of day, he thought he had a decent grip on everything. When the last horse was in its stall, fed and watered, and every employee had left, he shut down the computer. He'd just grabbed his thermos when Kinley paused at the open door.

"Looks like you survived your first day."

"Yeah. I got acquainted with the crew and some of the clients, and got familiar with some of organization and structure here."

He'd wondered if she'd be coming by to check on him. Try as he might, he couldn't ignore the country-girl appeal of her. Her pale blonde ponytail pulled through the back of her hat had curled into a heavy spiral, and he wondered what it would look like free and down her back. Even without makeup, her skin looked smooth and soft, her cheeks naturally flushed, and her large eyes blue as a summer Texas sky.

Back when he had two good arms, and when he was still in California, had he run into her in a bar, on the beach, or a hundred other places, he'd have talked her up and asked her out.

But she was his boss, and he didn't need a course in sexual

harassment in the workplace to recognize all the pitfalls of putting the move on her. Plus, if this job didn't work out, he'd need a reference for the next one. And a guy with a disability needed good references. He cut off the bitterness and turned his thoughts back to Kinley.

"I'm impressed with your water system. Those self-draining hoses will be great during cold weather."

"If they don't freeze. We haven't tested that out yet. Would you like to come with me and check out the other barn?"

"Sure. I want to take one last walk through before I leave things to Morgan for the evening."

She smiled. "I'll help."

AS THEY WALKED through, everything in Barn A looked just as she liked it. Wyatt seemed to have grasped the setup pretty comprehensively. The little ball of tension that had come and gone in her stomach all day finally relaxed and let go.

Once outside, he tossed his thermos into the front passenger seat of his SUV and got into her golf cart.

"I checked out the software you mentioned and called Keith about Tangerine."

He really was on top of everything. "What did he say?"

"That six months into her stay with them she started the behaviors you mentioned. It seemed to occur after she sustained an injury to her jaw. He said she settled back down after they bred her again, but she still nipped.

"Let's give her a couple of weeks to settle in with her filly, and then I'll start working with her and try to build some trust."

Kinley turned and rested an elbow on the back of her seat. "How do you plan to do that?"

"Patience, kindness, and observation. I have some remote camera equipment I brought with me from San Diego. I'm using the cameras right now to try and catch some..." He caught himself before saying assholes, "guys who've been cutting my dad's fences, but as soon as the cops have arrested them, I'd like to put one camera in Tangerine's stall and observe her behavior with all the staff. If we can find one worker she's more at ease with, it might ease the way for others. And I might be able to figure out what's triggering her. Would that be okay with you?"

Why hadn't she thought of that? "Yes, certainly. Anything to help her."

Kinley started the golf cart. The trip across the open field between the stables took only a minute, and she parked the cart at the door.

As they got out of the vehicle, she pointed to some of the similarities and some of the differences between the two stables, including the larger training ring. "That's where the therapy clients work with the horses. We do emotional therapy with the horses, as well as teach some of the clients to ride as part of their therapy, but the acceptance of their feelings and getting help to work through those feelings helps them the most.

"The horses are so attuned to human emotions, they can tell when someone is angry, upset, or sad. I've seen some amazing things happen in the ring.

"During their grooming sessions the kids address the events that are bothering them, and the repetitive movements soothe their anxieties and help them work through things.

"I want you to meet Walter. He's the star around here. He has a heart the size of Texas and the patience of Job. Nothing scares him. The loudest wheelchair, the screams when one of the clients is having a meltdown. He just keeps his composure and lets them hold onto him until they feel better.

"He sounds like a special horse."

"He is. A friend donated him to my program. She found him in a field, abandoned, abused, his hooves in horrible shape, and nearly starved to death. She rescued him but couldn't keep him. So, I took him, gave him TLC, built him back up, and now he's giving back."

She unlocked the barn door and pushed one side open.

"Was he part of the inspiration that led you to go into training therapy animals?"

"I suppose he was." She couldn't expect him to open up to her if she couldn't share things first. And she needed to know what kind of person he is since she was entrusting him with part of her life's work.

"At the same time I got him...my grandmother, my father's mother, was diagnosed with lymphoma." It was still hard to even say the words. "We all tried our best to help her through it, and for a while the treatments worked and we had hope she'd go into remission." She blinked rapidly against the tears. "When the treatments stopped working, the cancer spread." She swallowed against the pain and took a deep breath. "She died two years ago." She stood aside to let Wyatt enter. "Helping Walter fight his way back to health helped me accept that I hadn't failed Gran, because I didn't have the skills or weapons to fight her disease, but I did have skills to help him."

"You needed him and he needed you," Wyatt said.

"Exactly." They walked down the central aisle between the stalls. "I put an announcement about a lost horse in the paper for a month, just so I could say I'd done it, but the whole time it ran I was praying no one would claim him. It was a relief when no one did. I knew he was special the moment I started working with him."

"I have a special one at home, too. My Dad boarded my horse, Smoke, for me for years. When I could get leave to come home, I spent as much time with him as I did my family. Smoke and I are bonding again now, and I've been riding him every day. He's helping me adjust to life outside the Navy."

"What about therapy?"

"I had over a year of mandatory therapy. I don't go anymore."

He sounded more resentful than accepting.

She stopped before Walter's stall. The big bay wandered over and poked his reddish-brown head over the stall door. She ran a hand over the blaze on his forehead, but his dark ears came forward and he turned his attention to Wyatt. He seemed to study him.

Wyatt offered his hand palm down, and Walter sniffed the back of it, then eyed him again. Wyatt stroked his neck. "He's a beauty. Perfect markings, and at least sixteen hands. Why would anyone abandon him?"

"I thought maybe he'd gotten loose and just kept wandering. Or maybe they couldn't afford to feed him and they just turned him out. We have a few farms in the area who've had issues with underfeeding their livestock in the past."

Wyatt nodded. "And a fourteen-hundred-pound horse could eat you out of house and home. You don't have to worry about that anymore, do you, big guy?"

Walter stretched to sniff his shirt pocket. Wyatt chuckled and reached two fingers to fish out a peppermint. He unwrapped the treat and offered it to Walter from his palm. "The way he's studying me, it's like he's trying to figure me out."

"He probably is."

For the first time, Wyatt's usual reserve and control relaxed, and he turned his smile on her. She felt the warmth of it in places she tried hard to ignore.

A little flustered, she cleared her throat. "He likes the ladies. His current favorite is Katie Weber. She has Downs Syndrome. She's sixteen, small for her age, and stands maybe five feet tall. Her mother brought her here to help build her confidence and ease her anxieties. She was being bullied at school and unable to deal with it. Walter approached her as soon as she walked into the paddock, waited for her to pat him, and it was love at first sight for Katie."

"What happens when the client progresses and doesn't need therapy any longer?"

"They move on, and so do the horses. The animals are used to having people touch them, ride them, care for them. But they do have favorites. And they have good memories. Katie's one of Walter's favorites."

"I left Smoke for ten years, and every time I arrived home, he'd come racing across the field to see me."

She wondered about his life in California. "It's a shame you couldn't take him with you."

"Since I could be deployed at a moment's notice, or be gone for six months or more at a time... It was better for him to be here with my dad's staff."

She nodded. They wandered back toward the main entrance.

"Will you tell me about your arm injury, Wyatt?"

He was silent a moment. "My team and I were doing a fast rope down from a helicopter, and one of the guys lost his grip and fell. He wasn't a big guy, but we were both carrying fifty-pound packs plus our weapons... He grabbed my arm to try and save himself and ripped me off the line. If he'd fallen from that height and hadn't grabbed me, he'd have died. As it was, his velocity dislocated my shoulder and tore my rotator cuff and the tendons. Then we both dropped about fifteen feet to the ground, and I landed on my arm and dislocated my elbow.

"It wasn't the initial injury that caused the numbness and weakness. The surgeon popped my elbow back into place, but didn't check the nerve. By the time he realized he'd left the nerve constricted in my elbow.... He shook his head. "I had more surgery, but it hasn't improved things very much."

And now she understood the resentment and anger.

She locked the barn door and they got back into the golf cart.

"You've seen other specialists?"

"Three. Two discussed grafting the nerve to try and repair it, but if it didn't work, it might make the numbness and weakness in my forearm and hand worse."

"What happened to the doctor?"

"He was discharged from the military and is practicing in the public sector now."

Which didn't provide Wyatt with anything close to justice.

He fell silent for a beat. "I'm trying to move on."

"I hope working here can help you do that."

"Maybe it will."

She started the golf cart, backed out, and circled around to the parking lot.

When she pulled to a stop behind the gate, he turned in his

seat and focused on her. "Thanks for the tour, Kinley."

"I forgot to ask how your first day went."

He smiled, and once again she felt that tug of attraction.

"It was good. You've got good people."

"I think so too." She nodded. "Have a good evening."

"You, too." He opened the gate, then reached across to lock it for her before turning to walk to his car.

He might still have his Texas drawl, but he walked with a measured step she thought he probably got from his military training. And he sure looked good in those jeans.

Wyatt gave a wave as he pulled away, and she sighed. She could have invited him to dinner as a welcome to the business gesture. But it wouldn't have been just a gesture, it would have been asking for trouble. And she'd already had enough of that with Colter. Just thinking about Colter triggered a combination of bitterness, and embarrassment.

She was Wyatt's boss, and she needed to maintain some distance between them. But, damn, every time he smiled she wanted to jump his bones. And she'd learned the hard way that a charming smile could hide all sorts of darker things when it came to relationships. She needed to be careful. Colter hurt her pride, but she had a feeling Wyatt could hurt her much more if she got too close.

CHAPTER 7

SEAL TRAINING TAUGHT Wyatt to take nothing at face value with any mission. There were always unexpected things that cropped up. But what were the odds that during his first two weeks on the job, a worker would be injured in a four-wheeler accident and break an arm, and one of the horses would hit its knee on a branch during a ride and come up lame?

He reported both to Kinley after he worked things out with the schedule for the worker and called the vet for the injured horse. He'd certainly gotten a taste of what Kinley had been dealing with for years. An upset owner and the added responsibility of ensuring the horse received daily treatment for the injury increased the workload, not that much, but pile that on top of the seven years she'd been running the show…

He'd been semi-surprised that Kinley hadn't tried to micromanage everything, but instead kept her distance and allowed him to deal with it. In fact, after that first day he'd been the one to initiate contact between them.

Was it because she wanted to give him room to learn the ropes, or had he done something to put her off? He couldn't think of anything.

She'd obviously been better at blocking out thoughts about him than he'd been at blocking them out about her. Or maybe she decided to keep things all-business between them…probably a good idea for them both.

The drive back to his parents' ranch only partially relaxed him, and he'd attempted to shed the added tension by the time he pulled in under the carport, and was glad to see supper waiting on his porch with a note. *Hope you had a good week on the job. Love, Mom.*

She was taking his request for some space to heart. He found it both a relief and a point of guilt. He took the food inside and set it on the stove to reheat in a while. But first he bailed out of his boots and clothes, took a shower, and put on cargo shorts and a T-shirt, then discovered he was hungry enough to eat the lasagna out of his mother's casserole dish at room temperature, sitting at the island while sipping a cold beer.

He tucked his cell phone in one of the pockets of his shorts out of habit. He rarely got a call, and his teammates were still out of the country. He couldn't think about that.

He got another beer out of the fridge, hit the switch that activated the porch fans, and walked barefoot outside to settle into one of the Adirondack chairs. Wedging the beer between his thighs, he twisted the cap off with his right hand because he needed to rest the left one. Several times during the day a lancing pain had shot from his left elbow through his last two fingers. It was a pain in the ass. And set his anger off every time.

He nursed the beer while gazing at the purple haze hanging low in the sky as dusk tiptoed toward night. He liked this time of evening, when the late afternoon heat cooled some, and a small breeze kicked in from the direction of the bunkhouse, carrying the scent of fresh-cut grass and grilled meat.

In years past, while his grandparents owned the property, they'd run a full-time cattle ranch and had a bunkhouse of workers. Modern times had changed that. The ranch hands who lived on the property, four that he knew of, were bachelors, and those who were married had homes, wives, and kids close by.

He thought of Kinley and wondered how she'd managed both stables for so long by herself. The people who worked for her were certainly one of the keys, but her drive was what kept things going. Then to add the weight of the therapy patrons to the rest…

He shook his head. It must leave little time for her to have a life outside of work.

He understood that, since he'd been much like her while a SEAL. The period of inactivity after his injury had nearly driven him crazy. But he'd adjusted now. *Yeah, right.*

To have a full-time position gave him some purpose. And Kinley took him at his word when he said that he was up to the job. He looked at his left hand and closed and opened it. It was numb until the cramps hit. And typing on the computer keyboard was a challenge when he couldn't feel the keys.

But he'd faced worse challenges. *"The only easy day is yesterday,"* he murmured. He might not be doing what he loved, but he was doing something, and he was needed. He'd have to keep reminding himself of that.

He studied his left arm, the musculature less defined compared to his right... And his thoughts stubbornly returned to his boss.

Kinley'd already seen it. There were no surprises there for her. And she hadn't seemed repelled. She'd seemed more concerned about the scars on his shoulder. He traced the raised edge of the surgical scar through his T-shirt.

She was made of stronger stuff than most women, so maybe she wouldn't care if he was a little beaten-up.

Maybe he could bring up that trail ride she mentioned and get some alone time with her, away from clients, workers, and horses.

He knew deep down that it wasn't a good idea, but for the first time in what seemed like forever, he felt a stirring of interest in something beyond just getting through one day to get to the next. And that interest seemed to be her.

He yawned. Five-thirty still came just as quickly as it did in the teams. He picked up the half-empty bottle of beer and, finding it warm, poured the remainder over the side of the porch and took the bottle in to put in the recycling bin.

He was deep asleep when the alarm on his phone went off. Wyatt rolled to his feet in one move and reached for it. He opened the app, and though the image was a little dim, and both trespassers wore baseball caps, their faces were easily discernable. He watched as the two teenagers cut the fence and then moved out of range, farther into the pasture.

What the hell were they up to? So far none of the cattle had been taken, and they hadn't attempted to approach the nearby barn. Was it some kind of prank? They were risking their lives by approaching cattle on foot. Some of the steers could be aggressive and territorial.

While dragging on jeans and a sweatshirt, he dialed the sheriff's office. By the time he completed the call he'd put on heavy socks and shoved his feet into his boots. The dispatcher took down the location where he needed them to meet him where the fence was cut, at the intersection of the two county roads.

He kept an eye on his phone to see if the intruders were coming back to exit the property. Thirty minutes later a county sheriff's patrol car pulled up and two men got out and approached him, hands on their weapons.

"You called to report a trespass?" one asked.

"Yes." Wyatt offered his hand, "Wyatt Taylor. My dad owns this spread."

"Deputies Fischer and Becker." Fischer said, as Wyatt shook both their hands.

"This is the fourth time these guys have cut the fence and entered my father's property. We had some cattle get out on the road the last time, and they were nearly hit by a truck. Luckily, a neighbor spotted them and called, then waited until some of the men could come round them up and herd them back in the pasture. I've got photos and video footage of the trespassers." He called it up on his phone and turned the screen toward the two officers.

"Shit. We're getting these calls all over the county. They're high school kids climbing into pastures to ride the cows on a dare. One of them's going to get hurt. And we've already had a couple of reports of hurt animals."

"I brought my drone. If you're open to the idea, I can launch it and track them so we'll know when they're coming back out of the pasture. If they see the lights on the drone, it might make them rabbit. That way you won't have to sit out here all night waiting for them."

The two deputies grinned. "Sounds like a plan," Becker said. "You lead the way to where the fence is cut and we'll follow."

Wyatt got into his vehicle, and pulled off when he reached a wide area just beyond where the fence was cut. The deputies pulled in behind him, and one got out, then the squad car pulled away.

"Becker's going to look around and see if he can find their vehicle." Fischer said. "They couldn't have walked this far out."

Wyatt retrieved the drone from the back of his SUV, hit the on switch, and placed it on the ground. He plugged his phone into the remote and switched it on. The program quickly booted up and he toggled the drone straight up. He skimmed the top of a cluster of trees as he directed it northeast over the pastures. Cows came instantly into focus below its flight path.

A cramp suddenly rushed down from his left elbow, through his forearm and into his hand. He swore under his breath and gritted his teeth against the pain. He leaned back against the open hatchback of the SUV and braced the control against his thigh while maintaining control of the switch by using his thumb.

He tried to shift his focus to controlling the drone while pushing away the pain—not easy, since his fingers hurt like a sonofabitch. The drone caught quick movement on the right, and he turned the UAV in that direction.

Two young males came into sight. They'd already somehow mounted the cows and were attempting to stay astride them. He followed one's progress as he held on to the animal's ears and fought to keep his seat. The cow swung her head and bucked. The rider leaned too far to the side, tumbled off and face-planted.

Ouch.

Wyatt circled back to the other rider and came up above him and ahead of him. His face was clearly defined in the light.

"That's Howard Mullins' boy." Fischer said. "He's a straight-A student and a *cop's kid*. What the hell is he thinking?"

Wyatt shook his head. The kid wasn't thinking. "Peer pressure is a powerful thing."

"And one of them will get hurt, not to mention that twenty-five-hundred-dollar cow he's riding," Fischer grumbled.

Becker's voice came over the radio. "Fischer, I've found their vehicle quarter of a mile down, parked in some trees. It's registered to Howard Mullins."

"Stay with the vehicle in case they decide to cut the fence and cross over closer to the car. I'll let you know if they exit the pasture here. One of the trespasser's Mullins' oldest."

"Roger that."

"Wyatt turned his attention back to the kid riding the cow. The cow tripped and went down hard, chest first, and Mullins was flipped over her head. "Shit! That looked like it hurt," he commented.

"Yeah, it did." Deputy Fischer seconded.

The kid was getting to his feet, but the cow wasn't. Even as he watched, the cow kicked its leg and tried to get up, but fell back down. He caught a glimpse of the bottom half of her front leg flopping around, disjointed. His stomach pitched. "Shit, we have a cow down. It looks like she's broken a leg. I'll have to call Randall, our foreman." Wyatt reached for his phone and punched in the number.

"Yeah?" Randall's voice sounded slurred with sleep.

"Randall I'm up at the west pasture with the cops. We're waiting for our fence cutters to come out. They've been riding the cows, Randall, and we have one cow down. Her leg is broken."

"Damnit. I'm on my way."

Wyatt pulled the drone up and changed the angle so they could see both boys.

He followed the teen boys' progress with the drone as they climbed the hill to the road.

Fischer contacted his partner over the radio. "Becker, they're headed to the spot where they cut the fence. Call and get a tow for the car."

"Are you sure?"

"One of the cows is down and going to have to be euthanized."

"Roger that."

Becker pulled up in the squad car and got out. Ten minutes later the two boys hobbled out of the section of fence they'd cut.

Fischer clicked on his flashlight, spotlighting the two. Both boys jumped. "Freeze! Don't even think about running." He and Becker approached the two. Both looked bruised and battered. One had a bloody nose and was holding his T-shirt up over the lower half of his face. Fischer took young Mullins by the arm while Becker took the other teen. Neither one attempted to resist.

While Wyatt landed the drone and put it in the back of his SUV, the two officers searched and handcuffed the boys. Fischer explained to them they were being arrested for trespassing, destruction of private property, and injury to the cow. Then Becker read them their rights.

The two seemed subdued. Either their pride was hurt as bad as their bodies, or seeing the cow's injury had sobered them. They were probably also looking down the barrel of their parents' anger over this escapade.

Wyatt approached the deputies and the boys. "May I speak to them?" he asked.

"I don't think that's a good idea, Mr. Taylor." Becker said.

"I just want to know if these two are repeat offenders, or if this is the first time they've come up here to do this."

"Lucas?" Becker said.

The boy met his gaze. "This is the first time."

"I hope you'll be stand up guys and tell the deputies who else has come up here to ride cows. Otherwise, you two will be responsible for repairing the fence, and your parents for paying for it," Wyatt said.

"What about the cow?" The bloody-nose victim asked.

"There's no getting out of that one, guys."

The two hung their heads. "We never meant to hurt any of them," bloody nose said.

Wyatt thought of some of the stupid stuff he'd done as a

teenager. Most teenagers rebelled a little when they were growing up. These two would have to pay the price, and maybe they'd learn from it. Before they went too far and one of them paid the ultimate price like Logan had.

Randall drove up in his pickup and got out. The two deputies put the kids in the squad car.

"I didn't call Bryan," he said as he approached Wyatt. "I figure tomorrow morning would be soon enough to let him know about the cow. Where's she at?"

"I have GPS coordinates. We can drive right to her."

Deputy Becker approached him and handed him a card. "If you can email the video you took tonight to that email address, I'll do the paperwork to get it into evidence."

Wyatt nodded. "Will do."

"Thanks for your help," Becker said. He got into the patrol car and they pulled away.

"Okay, let's go," Randall said. "I'll drive you back to your car when we're done."

Wyatt walked to Randall's truck and opened the door. He'd killed in defense of his country and in defense of his teammates. And he'd eaten his fair share of steaks, burgers, ribs and beef stew. But he really dreaded what they had to do now.

CHAPTER 8

THE WEEKEND PASSED much too quickly. While her weekend crew took care of riders, she'd spent it weeding and spot-seeding a couple of the pastures, a job she'd meant to get to the month before.

Monday's therapy with Katie was usually relaxing because she had a good rapport with the young girl.

Kinley took the currycomb to Socks' side. The smaller horse was perfect for Katie to ride, but Walter was her true horse love. She didn't mind grooming Socks so Katie could groom Walter after their ride.

"Have you thought any more about inviting your father to watch you ride, Katie?"

Katie's confidence was growing by leaps and bounds. She rode today with confidence, and had done well. It was a real shame her father had never come here to see her.

"He won't come," Katie said. Her oversized tongue made every word she spoke sound like she was tongue-tied.

"Have you mentioned it to him?" Kinley asked.

"No."

"How do you know he won't come if you haven't asked him?"

Katie paid careful attention to what she was doing as she lifted Walter's huge hoof and picked the underside clean of debris. "He doesn't like me."

"That's not true, Katie. I don't think he'd pay for your therapy and riding lessons if he didn't care."

"He and my brother do things while I come here."

Would it be stepping over the line to call Sam Weber and fill him in on his daughter's progress? Maybe if he knew, he'd take an interest. She'd talk to Diane about it.

"What kind of things do you and your dad do together?" she asked.

"Watch television sometimes."

Great. Shit! "Maybe your father would like to learn to ride a horse like you have. Why don't you ask him?"

Katie moved on to the back hoof. "He won't."

"You'll never know unless you ask."

Silence fell between them while Katie finished up on Walter's hooves, then took out the face brush. She stood on a wooden block to groom Walter's long muzzle and cheeks. She paused to look into the horse's eyes and the two gazed at each other.

Kinley fought off sudden tears. When Katie was ready to move on, it was going to be difficult for her, but what about Walter? She'd wondered about that ever since Wyatt brought it up. Horses were so intelligent. She truly believed he'd sensed Katie's need for a friend and had purposely gone to her.

Kinley looked up to see Wyatt strolling toward them. Her heart seemed to do a tap dance every time she saw him. She just couldn't seem to shake the attraction. But if she acted on it and something soured between them, she'd be down one stable manager…or worse, he'd stick around and make things awkward.

"Hey," Wyatt greeted her then shifted his attention to Katie. "Hello."

Katie turned her head without looking at him. "Hello."

"You must be Katie," Wyatt said, surprising Kinley.

Katie looked down at her feet. "Yes."

"My name's Wyatt and Walter tells me you take very good care of him."

Katie laughed and peeked up at him. "Horses don't talk."

"Sure they do. You just have to listen." He cocked his head as though he heard something. "Walter says he wants a peppermint. Would you like to give him one?"

Katie grinned and her almond-shaped eyes tilted up at the corners. "Yes."

Wyatt offered her a hand down off the block. "I'll unwrap it, because the plastic wouldn't be good for him if he ate it. Now put your hand out, palm up." He demonstrated how she should position her hand.

Kinley had never seen Katie so at ease with an adult. She had completely forgotten to be self-conscious.

Katie stuck her short-fingered hand out straight. He dropped the peppermint on her palm. Walter's muzzle worked over her skin as he took the candy and Katie giggled. "That tickles." She rubbed her palm on her jeans.

"It does." He patted Walter's neck.

"Want to give Socks one?" he asked. "He might deserve a treat for letting you ride him."

Katie turned to Kinley. "Can I?"

Kinley nodded. "Sure."

She and Wyatt went through the same process again, and once again, the sound of Katie's giggles was something special.

"I saw you in the training ring," Wyatt said. "You and Socks make a good team. He's just the right size for you to ride."

"He is." Katie ran a hand down the long bridge of Socks's muzzle. "He doesn't get mad when I do something wrong."

"Horses are usually very patient. They know it takes practice to learn to ride." Walter nickered, and Wyatt said. "Walter says he's waiting for you to finish his grooming. Need help getting back up on the block?"

"No." Katie's smile held pride and her shoulders went back. "I can do it myself." She returned to Walter.

"While you work, I need to talk to Ms. Kinley," he said.

"Okay."

They stepped a short distance away.

In that moment, Kinley could hardly restrain the desire to kiss

Wyatt Taylor. "You are so good with her. Thank you."

"She seems a sweet kid."

"She is."

"I've sent a couple of the guys out to check the fences around your property."

Kinley's thoughts turned from a kiss to concern in a heartbeat. "Is there a problem?"

"There's a game the high school boys are playing. They're trespassing on people's property and riding cows. And even though you don't have cattle, I think it might be a good idea to check the fencing regularly, just in case."

"I think so too. Riding cows? Why would they want to do that?"

"It's a dare, and they're challenging other kids to do it. I caught two after they cut my dad's fence Saturday night, which has happened a few times in the past few weeks. The first group who got away with it must have told the others that my dad's spread is easy pickings. One of the cows broke a leg last night while one of the kids was riding her and had to be put down."

Kinley's anger rose. "That's… What time was this?"

"Saturday, at two in the morning." He dropped his voice. "One is a cop's son. And, needless to say, the dad is not happy. My dad had a meeting with the two boys' parents this morning. In exchange for not filing charges against them, the boys have to repair the fence, and the parents will pay for the fencing and the cow. And the boys have to bottle-feed the calf they left motherless until it's weaned. But I need a favor."

"Sure, what is it?"

"Both have had their cars taken away for the next six weeks, and they'll have to ride the bus home in the afternoons. They live just past Silver Linings. If we have an empty stall, I can bring the calf here, and they can feed it before they go to school, and get off the bus here to feed it again before going home. They'll have to clean up after it as well."

Kinley laughed. "How old is the calf?"

"It's two months old. I figure two months of having to feed

him every day should be punishment enough. What do you think?"

"Did you come up with this?" she asked.

"Yeah. I mentioned it to Dad before he went to the meeting this morning."

"I think it's brilliant. And they might just learn something as well."

Wyatt nodded. "Respect for animals and responsibility. Let's hope." He smiled. "Think it will be okay to turn the calf out in one of the small corrals close to the barn during the day?"

"Yeah, they'll have to go get him and bring him in after they feed him." She grinned. The two would be in for a treat. Calves butted their mothers to get their milk to come in. They'd do the same to the person feeding them a bottle.

"You said this was a game at the high school. Did they give the cops any information about any other participants?"

"No. But I think the Mullins kid's dad will keep working on him for answers."

"Good."

"Dad's giving me the beef since I caught them. When it's dressed, I'd like to have a barbecue and invite the staff to come out to the house and eat. Steak, ribs, and burgers."

Speechless for a moment she finally said, "Wow. That's very generous of you."

"Hey, what am I going to do with a whole cow? It's too early to give the meat away as Christmas gifts."

She laughed.

He touched her shoulder, and just that brief contact set needs alite. *What the hell is wrong with me?*

"I'll run the date by you before I pass out the invites."

"Okay."

"Better get back to work, or the boss lady might get after me for wasting time."

As she watched him walk away, she sighed.

"Elijah Pruitt and Carter Taft," Katie said from behind her, and she suddenly realized Katie been listening to their entire conversations.

"What about Elijah Pruitt and Carter Taft, Katie?"

"They bully me. They'd ride cows if they could."

If they were okay with bullying a defenseless girl, they probably would. "I thought your parents and the school counselor were working on stopping that."

Katie remained silent for a moment while she continued to brush "They still do it."

"Have you talked to your parents about it?" Kinley brushed the tangles out of Socks' mane.

"Daddy said to ignore them."

Why wouldn't that man step up for his child? She needed to talk to Diane, Katie's counselor. "Every time they bother you, report it to your teacher or the school counselor, *and* your parents. And tell Dr. Behr everything they say to you."

"I do."

She could read the hopelessness in Katie's face. It both broke her heart and enraged her. Katie was so defenseless against these boys. And so trusting and easily manipulated.

"Have Elijah and Carter ever hit you, Katie?"

"Carter shoved me, and I fell into the lockers."

"Did you tell your teacher?"

"He said it was an accident. He helped me up and said he was sorry."

Alarms were going off in Kinley's head. Because he'd been kind to her just once, she believed him. Or perhaps she knew the teachers weren't going to do anything about it, so she just went along to get by. These boys were eventually going to hurt her, seeing her as easy prey.

Wyatt was handling the two teenagers from last night in a productive way. He seemed to understand the mindset of teenage boys, probably because he'd been one. Her own experience as a teenager had been so totally different. She was a tomboy, strong from riding horses and working on the ranch. She wouldn't have had to tell a teacher. She'd have kicked their asses.

It was frustrating to her that Katie didn't know how to defend herself. And had trouble reading the cues telling her when she needed to.

"Katie, are there cameras in the halls at school?"

"I don't know."

Kinley would find out.

"Do you have a journal?"

"Yes." Katie moved the block around so she could step up on it, and used the curry brush on his side.

"Do you write about what happens at school in it?"

"Yes."

"Did you write about Carter the day it happened?"

"No."

"Why not?"

"Momma gets sad if I write bad things in my journal."

Kinley swallowed back a groan of frustration.

"Your mother loves you very much, Katie. She wants to know when things happen so she can keep you safe."

Katie remained silent a moment. "Okay." She looked up from putting away the grooming tools. "Mr. Wyatt said I did good riding Socks."

"Yes, he did. And Socks thinks so, too."

When Katie's mother arrived to pick her up, Kinley took her aside and told her what Katie had said about the boys. "I thought you'd want to know."

Mrs. Weber's eyes swam with tears. "I do, but I'm just about at my wits' end with this situation. We're thinking about moving Katie out of the high school, but she loves her teacher and any kind of change is difficult for her."

"I understand." But Katie needed to come first. "She was reluctant to tell you about the assault because she knew you'd be upset. I think Katie is more aware of the stress you and your husband are under than you realize.

"Do you know if the high school has cameras in the hallways?"

"Yes, they do."

"Why don't you talk to her and see if she'll tell you where she was when Carter knocked her down. The principal can pull up the footage and see if it was an intentional assault or the accident Carter claimed."

"That's a good idea."

"On a better note. Katie did very well with her riding lesson today. She's getting better control with the reins and she's gaining more confidence every week. And she's developed a good rapport with Socks. He's one of our most patient, laid-back mounts, and one of our smallest.

"I think she'd be thrilled if you and your husband would come one day and watch her ride."

"I'll come next week. But don't tell her. She tends to get anxious if she knows we're watching. She wants to please us so much."

And could never please her father, because he looks at her as an embarrassment and a bother. The woman didn't have to say it.

"I have a window in my office that looks out onto the practice ring. You can watch her from there, and even video her to show your husband." The asshole.

Mrs. Weber smiled for the first time. "I think that would be perfect. She'll be more at ease and less self-conscious that way."

As much as she loved her daughter, Adeline Weber came across as indecisive and weak-willed. If she wouldn't fight for her daughter, her husband definitely wouldn't.

A few minutes later as she waved good-bye to Katie as they pulled out of the parking lot, she couldn't shake the disheartening feeling that she'd failed her.

WYATT UNWOUND AN extension cord and plugged it into the outlet outside the two stalls. He opened the package of anchors he'd bought. The camera was triggered by motion and would drain the battery because the horse and her filly were seldom still. Plugging it in and letting it run twenty-four seven would be a better option.

Kinley's buckskin mare Indira watched him with interest as he ran the cord along the top of the stall with stick-on anchors and pulled the small zip ties to hold them in place. He secured the plug to the rafter with duct tape, attached the camera, and turned it on.

His phone signaled the camera was live, and he opened the app to a real-time image of Tangerine and her baby. While mama ate some hay from the wall feeder, the baby nursed. He smiled at the peaceful, domestic moment. The mare seemed to be settling into motherhood without a hitch.

He climbed down the ladder and Indira approached him. She was a beautiful horse, her muzzle, ears, mane, tail and the lower half of her legs were dark, and the rest of her a golden tan color, a perfect example of buckskin coloring. "I don't have any peppermints, girl. Just a pat or two," he said as he stroked her.

"She's taken to you," Gerald said from the stall door. "Six months ago, she wouldn't have let you in her stall. She was a little afraid of men."

"I'm glad to see she's over that."

"We all are. Kinley's waiting to speak with you. She's in your office."

Just once he'd like for her to want to speak to him about something other than business. But if she did... Knowing about his arm and seeing the adjustments he had to make because of it firsthand would probably turn her off. After nearly a year of avoiding women because of his arm, he needed to get his head right before jumping into anything.

"I'll put the ladder up and see what she needs."

"I can do that," Gerald said, opening the stall door.

With a murmured thanks, Wyatt strode down the barn to the office. He searched Kinley's face as he walked in. Her cheeks were flushed and there was tension in her face. "Something wrong?"

"I want to thank you again for the way you responded to Katie today. Your compliment about her riding thrilled her."

"I noticed how hard she was trying, and it never hurts to offer encouragement." He hiked one hip on the corner of the desk. "Are you okay?"

She hesitated. "It's just...when you know about a volatile situation and you pass along the information to the one person you expect to take action...." She looked away. "I'm not really supposed to discuss the therapy patients...."

"Give me a hypothetical situation," he suggested.

"Say a young girl, a teenager who functions on a seven-year-old level, is being bullied, and she's identified the boys, but her mother seems more interested in her own trials in dealing with it than what they might do to protect Katie."

He was learning that Kinley would give of herself to the point of breaking. She needed to learn to pace herself.

"Hypothetically...what would you do if you were her mother?" he asked.

"My first instinct would be to grab the little shits by the ears, drag them out of the school, and beat the crap out of them."

He laughed, then sobered. "What would be your second instinct?"

"To call the principal and set up a meeting with him, her therapist, her teacher, and the parents of the boys who are bullying her. They've already done that, but it hasn't worked. The little shits keep getting away with it."

She began to pace, her expression set, her eyes alight with emotion. "Her mother is ineffective in the way she deals with the school, she's a meek personality. Her father has told Katie to just ignore the boys, but one shoved her into a locker recently then told her it was just an accident. She's easily manipulated, and she's not aggressive enough to defend herself."

Wyatt slipped off the desk and caught her arm. "Hey, take a breath for a minute." It came natural as breathing for him to cup her cheek with his left hand. He couldn't feel the warmth of her skin, or the texture as his palm rested there and he regretted bitterly that the first time he touched her he couldn't feel her skin.

Her gaze locked with his. Her pupils dilated, leaving only a narrow rim of light blue. She moistened her lips with the tip of her tongue. A wild, pulse-pounding desire to snuff out that regret by bringing her in close and feeling how her body fit against his reared up. He wanted to taste her lips, her skin.

It had been over a year since he'd held a woman. Just as long since he'd been intimate with one. And at the moment he was very aware of both.

He brought his right hand up to cup her other cheek. Her skin was warm, and she smelled of hay, and, underneath that, a more feminine scent. Her fingers curled over his wrist, but she didn't pull away.

A knock came at the door, and he reluctantly dropped his hands and took a step back. "Come in."

Gerald poked his head in the door. "Your dad's foreman called and said they'll transport the calf tomorrow before three."

"Okay."

Gerald looked back and forth between them before he shut the door.

Wyatt searched for something to say and managed, "What did you suggest to Katie's mother?"

"That she ask the principal to view camera footage from the hallway where he shoved, Katie to prove it was on purpose."

"That's a good plan. And let's hope Mom follows through with it. And as much as you want to do something to help, you can't overstep the professional boundaries. They might pull Katie from your program. And that would devastate her and upset you."

"Yes, it would. I need to get off to a good start with this." Kinley leaned back against the desk and stared at the wooden floor.

"In SEAL training, you learn to distance yourself from the human elements of a mission, so you can see things dispassionately and maintain your focus. I'm not saying you need to go that far, but you need to protect yourself, Kinley, and your business. You're Katie's confident and her support, but at the end of the day, it's up to her parents to protect her."

"You're right."

They were both subdued. And after that moment of intense need, Wyatt searched for a way to come back to it in some way. "You're brave to take this on. It's not easy, but you'll find your way."

She looked up. "Is that what you're doing, Wyatt? Finding

your way?"

"Yeah, pretty much. It's taken me eight months to get this far, and it's been a year since my surgery." Eight months since his teammates left the country without him. He'd grieved and raged against the injustice of it, but in the end, he had to accept it.

She looked up. "I can only guess how hard it's been."

She had too much empathy for her own good. And he certainly didn't want her pity. "You stepped into your grandparents' footsteps and took on this place and added to it. That couldn't have been easy."

"But I didn't have to start from scratch."

Maybe he didn't have to either. He just needed to take things slow, and make certain she wanted the same thing he did. She was already taking him into her confidence. He suddenly experienced a rush of anticipation similar to when he stood at the door of an aircraft preparing to leap out. "What do you do when you're not working, Kinley?"

"Sleep."

They both laughed. "I'm going to bring my drone to work tomorrow, and after we lock up, I'll show you how to fly it?"

She cocked her head to the side as she studied him. "Why would you do that?"

"Because I think you'd enjoy doing something new, something you haven't tried before. Something fun." Something not related to horses and the business.

"I think I'd like that, too." She straightened from leaning against the desk. "I'd better go."

He allowed himself to study her trim waist and hips and the tight, spiraled curl of her ponytail that fell mid-back as she walked to the door.

She looked back over her shoulder, "Thanks for letting me vent."

"Any time."

When she flashed him a smile at the door, he felt the weight of it arrow right to his groin. If he was reading things wrong, it would be embarrassing as hell, but he didn't think he was.

CHAPTER 9

WYATT WIPED HIS brow with a bandana and paused at the outside boot-scraper to clean the horse manure off his boots. When she first hired him, Kinley warned him about one of the stallion's feisty behaviors. The horse had damn well been in fine fettle this morning when Wyatt arrived to discover one of the mares had come in heat. Arrow had been calling to her all morning and had decided to try and kick through his stall door.

It took him and Gerald twenty minutes to get the stud out of the stall and placed in a pasture far from the barn for the day. Then they'd transfer him to Barn B until the mare was no longer a distraction.

Wyatt could feel the tension in Barn A as soon as he stepped inside. After a quick scan, he spied Hunter Wagner standing a couple of feet from Tangerine's stall.

Kyle Stahl, one of their part-time workers, sidled up. "He arrived ten minutes ago. Real friendly guy. He didn't seem too happy about you being here running the place, Mr. Taylor."

"It's okay, Kyle. I'll handle him. Just go ahead with your work."

He wandered down the barn to where Hunter stood outside Tangerine's stall.

"Hello, Hunter." Wyatt said as he approached him. He glanced in to make certain all was well with the pair. Tangerine and the filly huddled in the corner of the stall. Tangerine's ears were back and her attention focused on the stall door.

"You lied to me about working here," Hunter said as he turned his attention to him.

"No. I didn't. I wasn't an employee when we ran into each other. But after you mentioned it, I thought I might like working here. So, I applied for a job. I started a few weeks ago."

"Why did you leave your dad's spread?"

"I'm not needed on the ranch. And I've always been more interested in horses than cattle."

"Being in the Navy doesn't really qualify you to work here!"

"No. But my experience as a Petty Officer in the Navy doesn't limit my abilities or knowledge in any number of areas, any more than your abilities as a lawyer limits yours." Wyatt studied the man's face. What about his presence in Kinley's stables had him worked up? "Have you ever owned a horse before, Hunter?"

"No."

"Ever ridden one?"

"No."

"Kinley gives riding lessons."

"I've never been interested in riding."

"Then why own a horse?"

"It was a good investment, because a lot of my clients are cattle and horse people."

Wyatt nodded. He could picture Hunter sucking up at parties, dropping the line that he had a horse. A beautiful chestnut thoroughbred and she just birthed a filly. "Are you going to invest in cattle too?"

"I have some investments in a couple of cattle ranches in the area. Think your dad would be interested in an investor?"

Wyatt suppressed a laugh and controlled his expression with an effort. "He's always been a one-man show, but you can ask him."

"Maybe I will."

"If you have any questions about Tangerine or the filly, just let me know."

Hunter pointed toward the feed schedule. "Why have you changed Tangerine's feed?"

He had a feeling Hunter asked more to test him than because he wanted to know. "She's lactating and producing about three gallons of milk daily, so she'll naturally need to eat more calories and drink more water so she can feed the filly. Lactating mares need to eat between two to three percent of their body weight in hay and feed each day. Mare's milk is high in protein, so the foal gets what it needs. Tangerine's eating more for two now than she was while she was pregnant. Along with grazing, she's also receiving appropriate amounts of vitamin supplements to ensure her milk supply is healthy, and to ensure she maintains a healthy weight and constitution. We'll have to do this for the next four or five months, until the filly is weaned." By the time he'd finished explaining, Hunter's eyes had glazed over with disinterest.

A new client came in, and Wyatt took the opportunity to excuse himself to go greet her and introduce himself. But he kept his attention on Hunter. The man never stepped close to the door again, and he left the barn after only a few minutes.

Wyatt wandered back down to Tangerine's stall. She and the baby were still in the corner, as far away as she could get from the door. Wyatt strode down the barn to his office and went in. He stopped the camera feed and slid it back to where Hunter arrived at the door.

The mare became agitated and paced back and forth, almost stepping on her filly, but the baby was quick to get out of the way. Hunter stepped back from the door, and Tangerine's agitation eased, but her ears remained back and her attention remained focused on the door.

She might have nipped at different people who worked with her, but Wyatt had never seen her so agitated before, not even when the male staff entered the stall.

It seemed Tangerine didn't like Hunter any more than he did. In fact, she appeared frightened of him. A sick feeling curled inside his belly.

He needed to be sure to be present the next time Hunter visited and observe her interaction with him. There was a real possibility she might accidentally step on the filly or crush her against the stall wall if she got too worked up.

He made a note of where on the feed the video was, ran past that section, and turned the camera on again. He'd show the video to Kinley later and see what she thought.

He wanted Kinley's attention on something other than her clients, but when he brought this to her attention, she was going to be upset.

He'd need to show her today after work, and get it out of the way.

WHY WAS SHE seesawing between excitement and uncertainty at spending time with Wyatt? It was what she wanted. And it was too late to waffle now. She'd already said yes.

He worked one barn and she worked the other, so there wasn't that much contact between them during the day, since their jobs were separate. So if something went wrong... She might not lose him as a manager.

Why was she being negative from the get-go? On second thought, that was a dumb question. Colter had shaken her ability to trust. But worse, he'd shaken her confidence in her ability to judge anyone's character, and her ability to fully depend on anyone.

And lusting after Wyatt from afar was totally different from actually acting on it.

Then why had she taken Wyatt into her confidence about Katie?

Because there was a rock steadiness about him. He'd lost a friend who was close to a brother to him, and he was still able to move on and become a SEAL.... How much mental and physical courage had that taken?

Then he'd lost his SEAL career and partial use of his arm, and he was still moving forward.

Was she reading all that wrong?

Surely not.

This was just an hour flying a drone. It didn't have to mean more.

But the way he looked at her for those few moments... Like she was a popsicle and he'd been out in the dessert for a week dreaming of one. She'd felt that look to her toes.

She sighed. She still had work to do and only an hour to do it in. The low of a calf came to her before she ever reached the barn. He was not happy, or he was hungry, or both.

She went to the stall to look at the calf. Cows were so plentiful in Texas, she'd seen plenty of them and been around them since birth. And every baby was cute to a certain degree. But the hundred twenty or so pound two-month-old Hereford intimidated her a little since he weighed more than she did.

The boys were in for a battle.

Gerald wandered in while she was studying the calf. "I heard our new arrival was here and was curious. Why are we keeping a calf?"

"It will only be for a couple of months. It's a lesson in empathy and respect for animals." She gave him a rundown of the whole situation.

Gerald shook his head. "Damn fool kids. My parents would have tanned my backside and sent me to work on the ranch for the summer, and my pay would have gone to pay for the cow."

"Working on the ranch would have been a good idea if it was already summer break."

"It will be in a couple of weeks," he offered.

"It will, won't it? You should mention that idea to Wyatt."

He raised one shoulder. His brows forked into a frown. He was two years younger than she was, but looked older somehow. He wasn't as muscular as Wyatt, but he was nearly as tall. His dark brown eyes sometimes transitioned almost to black, depending on his mood. "Once Wyatt settles in a little more...I'd like to move to Barn B, Kinley."

A dropping sensation struck her stomach. She'd hoped the

separation would deter him. He'd asked her out periodically, but she always turned him down. "We have more horses over there to care for, Gerald, and you're familiar with them all. Once summer really hits and the tourists start rolling in, I'll need you to do more trail rides, and you'll be over here more often. But the boarding part of the operation is the year-round, steady income for us. Especially with the number of full-service clients we have." And most of them were full-service.

"Because the horses over here are groomed by the therapy patients, I don't need as much help. You're where I need you to be."

And he was where she wanted him. He was a valuable part of her team, and she'd done everything to keep their relationship on a business footing, but he wanted more. More than she wanted to give him.

"You get along well with Wyatt, don't you?"

"Yeah. He knows what he's doing. But he isn't you, Kinley." He looked at her for a long moment, and for the first time she saw anger in the darkening of his eyes and the tension around his mouth. When he turned and walked away, she was both relieved and uncomfortable.

At three-thirty on the nose, the two teenagers and Wyatt wandered into the barn. Wyatt had the boys carrying the hundred-pound bag of powdered milk replacement between them, while he carried a bucket with two nursing bottles in it, a gallon storage jar and a gallon of milk. "Boys, this is Ms. Green. She owns the stables and has agreed to house the calf until you've finished this learning experience." Wyatt winked at her. "Ms. Green this is Tyler Mullins."

Tyler was tall for sixteen but thin as a wire. His blond hair was buzz-cut close to his head and shone even in the dull lights of the barn. He was sporting a bruise along one cheek and a scratch over his eye.

"This is Greg Young."

Greg was chunkier, and had a black eye, a red nose, and a wild rash of freckles that exaggerated the injuries he'd sustained.

"Where would you like them to store this?" Wyatt asked about the bag.

"In the storage room. We have running water in there, so you can use warm water to mix the milk."

"You'll want to supplement the milk replacer with whole milk. Otherwise your calf will lose weight instead of gain it." Wyatt said.

"There's a fridge in the storage room. We use it to store meds, and the employees put their lunches in there."

Wyatt nodded. "I'll supply the whole milk. It will be in that fridge. You'll be subsidizing his diet with roughage and grains as well—since his mother isn't around to supply him with the nutrition he needs. After he eats in the morning, you'll take him out to one of the pastures so he can forage during the day while you're at school, then you'll go out and bring him back in to feed him after school. Since he has no mother or herd to protect him, he'll have to stay in the barn at night." The whole time Wyatt was speaking the calf was lowing.

"Why is he doing that? He's so loud!" Greg said.

"He thinks he's lost. He's calling for his mother," Wyatt said.

The two teens looked down.

"We've also had to separate him from the rest of the herd in order for you to feed him and care for him. Your parents decided the trip out to the ranch was too far to drive to and from each day."

"Who'll look out for him during the day?" Tyler asked.

"We have a small pasture we'll keep him in, where he'll be safe and within sight of the staff here," Kinley said.

"Bring that bag, and I'll teach you how to mix up some milk for him," Wyatt instructed. "We'll see if he'll drink from a bucket. If he won't, we'll have to use the bottles."

Kinley shook her head as Wyatt led the boys into the storage room and the sink. He was piling it on thick to make the boys feel guilty, as they should. Making it about the cow and her calf plucked the heart strings and might possibly teach the boys empathy.

In reality, if the cow produced healthy calves, she might have lived on the ranch for several years before being killed. But eventually she would have been sent to slaughter. Such was the life of cattle ranching.

While Wyatt supervised the boys, she went into her office to schedule the farrier for the next week.

After about half an hour, Wyatt appeared and knocked on the open door.

"Come on in." As soon as he stepped into the room she asked. "How'd it go?"

"He almost knocked Greg down butting the bottle."

She laughed.

"I took pity on them, and we put the calf in the pen out back so he could nurse from the bottle from between the slats."

"So, he wouldn't drink from the bucket."

"No. We could have possibly gotten another cow to take him…"

"But then it would have let the kids get off too easily."

"Yeah. I think they might both get attached after four weeks of this, and it might be a wrench when we return the calf to the herd."

"Another learning experience for them. Let's hope the two of them don't decide to become vegetarians," Kinley muttered.

Wyatt chuckled. "On the other hand, they may appreciate a good hamburger a little more after they get a taste of how much work goes into cattle ranching. I appreciate you allowing me to do this here. The commute out to the ranch was inconvenient for the parents."

"No problem. Gerald had a good idea about this whole learning experience. He suggested having the boys work on the ranch and having their salary pay for the cow."

"Wish I'd thought of that myself, but then someone would have to supervise them while they were there and be responsible if one of them gets hurt."

"That's true. But it was a good idea."

"I'll keep it in mind in case anything like this happens again. I installed the camera over Tangerine's stall, and I'm checking the video off and on during the day, every time one of the staff goes into the stall or opens the door. I'll let you know what I think. I can already tell you she's more at ease with women than men."

"Not surprising since we're smaller, less of a threat."

He nodded. "I thought I'd assign Carol to take care of her. She's soft-spoken and really knows how to approach the horses. She should be good with Tangerine."

"She would be." She'd have chosen Carol herself. Wyatt really had gotten a handle on things quickly.

"I thought the calf could use some time out to graze, so I left him in the pen. I have feed for him out in my car. I'll bring it in and I'll go out and get him and bring him in before I leave for the night."

"I can do that."

"My dad's calf, my responsibility. Besides, cows can be stubborn, and he's bigger than he looks."

He didn't have to say more about that. "Okay."

"There's just one other thing."

Something in his tone had eyes gaze leaping to his face.

"The video camera in Tangerine's stall caught something today I think you should see."

She got up from her seat. "Let's see it."

"I made a copy and transferred it to my phone."

He opened an ap on this phone and handed it to her. Tangerine paced back and forth, nearly stepping on the baby. Hunter Wagner was barely visible at the door. When he stepped out of sight the horse calmed, but still stood protectively close to the baby, with her ears back and her eyes on the door.

She watched the video twice, and both times her heart was in her throat at how close the mare had come to trampling the filly. She felt almost sick. "She's terrified of him. What alerted you to it?" She handed him the phone. Her legs shook with reaction and she had to lean back against her desk.

"She never changed posture for as long as he was there. I think she would have charged him if he'd stepped inside the stall. The longer she remained that way, the more uneasy I felt."

It took all her willpower to fight back the tears. "We can't deny him access to her. He's her owner."

"I know. But we can change where he sees her so she won't be trapped inside a confined space. At least that way the filly will be safer. I think he realized she was about to injure the baby and backed off.

"He's purchased her as an investment, and the filly will probably be sold as soon as it's weaned. I'll make an excuse to put her in the small pasture with the filly when he comes. That way Tangerine can move away from him when she needs to."

She looked up. "And once the filly is sold or separated from Tangerine?"

"We can't do anything until we catch him in the act. But the jaw injury Tangerine sustained at Keith's… If it wasn't just an accidental injury…he had to have struck her with something. I'll call Keith in the morning and discuss it directly with him. Maybe he'll be willing to share something with me in confidence."

Kinley walked around her desk and sat down, then pressed her shaking hands between her knees. She struggled to control a wave of anger so strong it nearly choked her. "Why would he hurt her?"

"He's a bully. He was one in high school, and I'm sure he's always been. She's bigger than he is, but he still has power over her. Physically abusing her would be the ultimate affirmation of that."

Tears ran down her cheeks, and she brushed them away. "You don't think he was beating her while she was pregnant, do you?"

"I doubt it. I'm sure Keith's people were keeping a close eye on her. That may have been why he moved her."

"He was thinking we wouldn't notice anything. Do you think he may have abused her after she lost the colt?"

"Maybe so. You said he moved her almost immediately after the colt died. And right after that was when she sustained an injury."

Kinley nodded.

"Look, Kinley, you didn't miss anything. You noticed the

change in her behavior as soon as he moved her back and called my attention to it."

That only helped alleviate her guilt a little. "If we're too obvious about keeping her away from him, he may try to move her again."

"I'll make up excuses to keep her and the baby outside as much as possible. Stress the filly's health and wellbeing. Which is true. If he can't corner her, he can't harm her."

"But that means we'll need to monitor her and the baby while they're outside. I've been meaning to upgrade our security. I'll buy a system and have it installed." Having something proactive she could do made her feel better.

"You'll need to be careful with the camera placements so he won't notice them." Wyatt cautioned. "He didn't notice the camera I installed because I set it up in Indira's stall and pointed it down into Tangerine's. I've had Tangerine and the baby put out in the pasture until she settles back down. While she's out, I'll check and make sure he can't see the camera from inside the stall, just in case."

"Good." She drew a deep breath. "Thank you for all of this, Wyatt."

"You're welcome."

"Since you know more about security systems, I'd like you to walk around with whoever I get to come out."

"I can do that. I'll call Keith and see when he can meet with me. Maybe away from both barns would be best."

She nodded. "Probably so."

"You have any lawn chairs around here?" he asked.

"Yeah, why?"

"I brought a six pack of beer and I thought we could order some takeout after we finish flying the drone."

She was tempted to cancel their plans. He was probably half way expecting it. Something in the level look he gave her made her change her mind. "We don't have to tailgate here. You can drive over to the house and we'll eat out on the back deck. It's covered and lovely during the evening."

"Okay." The quick smile he flashed her set off flutters in her stomach. "I'll see you after work."

Once he left, she got on the computer to research security systems and companies.

CHAPTER 10

WYATT WENT DIRECTLY to Tangerine's stall and moved around the space to see where the camera was visible. He collected the ladder from the storage room, made some adjustments to the camera's position, and worked to better hide the electrical cord with tan duct tape. He returned the ladder and went in to check on Jet, the injured gelding.

After applying ice packs on and off the day of the injury, they had been administering the anti-inflammatory the vet prescribed, the horse seemed more comfortable. He checked the wrappings to make certain they weren't too tight, gave the good-natured horse a pat or two, and moved on to the next thing, calling Keith Myers to see if they could meet in the next couple of days.

He left a message on the answering machine for him to return his call, leaving his cell phone as the call-back number.

The last hour of the day seemed to drag, and by the time he and his team had the horses stalled, fed, and watered, he was eager to leave. He swung by Tangerine's stall one last time and rested his left arm atop the door. She eyed him with suspicion and refused the peppermint he offered her.

Because of the abuse, she might never trust anyone completely ever again. Which was a real shame. He left the candy on the top of the door and went to check the back door. She'd wandered over and was munching the candy by the time he went past to the front.

He took a few minutes in his office to shuck his boots and put on running shoes, evidence of his run-in with the stallion earlier in the day still clinging to the boots, as well as the smell.

He said goodnight to Morgan Baumman, one of the part time workers who stayed until eight and once outside, he turned his attention to the evening ahead and left the rest behind. Seeing Kinley's golf cart was already gone, he got in his vehicle and drove around to her driveway. The paved road wound back into a stand of trees and opened up to a large, nicely manicured yard surrounding a long ranch-style house with a porch across the front. A porch swing with colorful pillows hung at one end. Three cane-bottomed rocking chairs were lined up in an equidistant pattern at the other end.

Kinley sat in one of the rocking chairs, her hat gone, but her ponytail still in place. Wyatt parked in the drive and opened the door. He moved around the back of his car to open it and retrieve the cooler.

"Are you a runner, Wyatt?" Kinley asked as he mounted the steps.

"Five miles a day before work."

The surprise on her face made him smile. "Old habits die hard. Arrow was pissed that I relocated him today and decided to take a dump on my feet to show his displeasure." He placed the cooler close and opened it. He took out two cold bottles of beer and handed her one. "I thought I'd give us both a break from the smell of manure."

She laughed. "He's a beautiful stud, but he's also a *primo uomo*."

"Is that what you call it? I had a few more succinct things to call him this morning and this afternoon, and I ended up leaving my boots in my office. I'll scrub them down after I get to work tomorrow." He took a seat in the rocker next to hers.

"Are you really settling into the position as easily as you seem to be?"

"It isn't that much different from what I've done on my father's spread. Adjusting to a schedule isn't the hard part."

"What do you find the hard part?"

"Having to be social. On dad's spread, the only things you talk to are the cows or the horses. At the barn I'm always running up against those pesky humans."

She laughed. "Your team seems to have accepted you pretty easily."

"Gerald smoothed the way by accepting me. He could have run the show." He turned from studying the distant hills to look at her. "Why didn't he take the leap?"

"He doesn't want to have to deal with the paperwork, vet, farrier, suppliers, and all the scheduling or the few difficult riders we have. He'd rather just come to work and deal with the horses."

Wyatt could understand that.

She changed the subject. "Is California very different than Texas?"

"The land, not so much. There are hills, desert, forest, brush, as well as coastal and plains areas, just like Texas. We trained in the desert a lot, and on the coast in the water, of course. And at least the water in the Gulf is a helluva lot warmer than the Pacific Ocean." But he missed watching a sunset against the backdrop of the ocean. Missed the camaraderie of the brotherhood, missed always having something new to learn. But there'd also been boredom at times. And he certainly didn't miss dodging bullets.

"Did you leave anyone important behind when you left, Wyatt?"

Only his team. "No. I wasn't seeing anyone when I left. Being in the military is hard on relationships. The separations are tough." And he'd had a lot of separations, He took a deep drink of his beer.

"That sounds lonely."

"Sometimes." He decided to turn the tables. "What about you?"

"I kicked my last to the curb. I bought into his charm and discovered there was nothing behind it. He said I thought more of the horses than I did of him, and in the end I had to agree." Her tone held more anger than bitterness.

"Excuses, excuses," Wyatt murmured. She turned wide blue eyes in his direction. "What did he ever do for you to earn the attention he thought he deserved?"

She was silent for a moment that stretched into two. A smile started to spread across her face until she threw her head back and laughed. "Obviously not as much as he thought he had. That's one of the best lines I've ever heard."

He buffed his fingernails on his shirt and she laughed again.

"Where's the drone you've been telling me about?"

"In the back of my car. I'll get it." He set his beer down on the porch and rose from the rocking chair.

He was down the steps when she said his name and he turned to look up at her. She stepped down to him and stood on one step above him making them nearly eye to eye. She rested her hands on his shoulders and kissed him, a soft, sweet kiss with just a touch of heat. He wasted no time in curving his good arm around her and rested his hand against the small of her back, holding her, while he kept his weak arm at his side.

"That's for what you did for Katie the other day."

She kissed him again and moved in close. His body responded enthusiastically. Her lips parted, inviting more. She tasted like the beer, but also like her, spicy and warm. When she drew back, her eyes were dark and her cheeks flushed. "That's for that perfect line."

"I'll try to come up with another before I leave," he teased, his voice husky.

She smiled and withdrew her arms. With a sigh of regret, he released her and went to the car for the drone.

The house had the open-floor plan of a new renovation, much like his cabin. Kinley led the way from the wide foyer just inside the front door, through the living room-kitchen combination done in a kind of light grayish-green and white, with overstuffed chairs, oak tables, and a sofa big enough to divide the room into two separate spaces. The place wasn't huge like his mom and dad's house, just comfortably spacious, with an easy, welcoming feel to it.

She opened one side of double French doors that led onto a covered deck stretching the length of the house. He walked across the deck and looked toward the stables. One of the large pastures ran the length of the property and seemed to roll toward the distant hills. She seemed isolated here. "When you have the stables wired, you might want to have some kind of alarm system put in the house as well."

She frowned and looked off into the distance toward the stables.

She'd never had an animal abuser as a client. He didn't want to say it and spoil the mood. He kept his tone casual. "It wouldn't hurt to have some security around the house since you can see it from the stables."

He placed the drone on one of the tables. "We'd better fly while we still have light. It takes some practice to fly at night."

"How often do you fly this?"

"My teammates and I used to fly them on the weekends. I hadn't flown this one in over a year until the other night. I tracked and filmed the boys after they cut the fence and came onto my dad's property. And I got their ride on the cows."

"Did you fly them in the Navy?"

"Yeah. Armed and unarmed UAVs. That's Unmanned Aerial Vehicles. We used them for reconnaissance mostly, but also for extra firepower if we needed it.

"This one is a tactical drone and it can take video or still photos, or just fly."

She moved close beside him. "Show me."

He unfolded the drone's four flying mechanisms and took the cover off the camera gimbal and put it in his pocket. Next he plugged his phone into the controller, opened the operating system app, and turned the controller on. The controller beeped as it finished its booting process.

"This left stick controls the altitude of the drone. If I push it forward it will go up, backward it will go down. To the left or right, it will send the drone left or right, but it stays within the hovering altitude you've already established. The right stick controls the forward, backward, right, or left flight of the drone.

"I'm going to set it at its slowest speed so you can practice flying it."

Kinley shook her head. "First I want to watch you do it."

"Okay." He pushed the *on* button on the drone, it ran through its boot-up process, and then its propellers began to turn. Wyatt fit the left stick in the groove between his thumb and the widest part of his hand. He pushed the left stick forward, and the drone rose in the air and hovered about eight feet up. He demonstrated how to direct the UAV to the left or right slowly with the left stick. The flight forward and backward was easier to control because he could feel the stick in his right hand and didn't have to be so cautious about the pressure. He sent the drone forward into the pasture, then turned it slowly around and brought it back to land on the table."

"You make it look so easy."

"It just takes muscle memory and practice. Be sure to remember that if you turn the drone around to bring it back, everything will be backwards on the right stick. So right will be left and back will be forward.

"Just practice moving the sticks first and get a feel for it. It's set at a slow speed so you can get used to it, and so the video you film has a more cinematic feel to it." He Handed her the control.

Kinley sat down in one of the cushioned deck chairs and pushed the left stick so the drone rose to ten feet. She concentrated on the left and right movement. "I bet you didn't use the slow speed with your teammates."

"No. But this isn't the first drone I've owned, either. Or the second or the third. With competition comes crashes. We finally got too much money invested and started doing other competitions. Like who got the best shot of wildlife, or a sunset, or a panoramic view." Or the babes on the beach, but he wasn't going to tell her about that. "Or the most embarrassing moments videos."

"And what did that consist of?"

He laughed. "I've been sworn to secrecy, but drink may have been involved."

She laughed. "I can only imagine. Guys seem to have a talent for creative craziness."

"That's one way of putting it." A feeling akin to homesickness crowded his chest. He turned his attention to Kinley to fight it off.

She had caught on quickly and was flying the drone back and forth across the pasture.

"How high can it fly?" she asked.

"Four hundred feet is the legal limit. Manned flights start at five hundred feet, so you can't go any higher."

"And what about the distance?"

"For this particular drone, four miles."

She took her eyes off the screen for a moment. "Can I try and fly it to the barns and back?"

Since it was pretty much a straight shot there and back, he thought she could do it. But the light was going, and the grayish purple of evening was coming down fast.

"You'll need to turn the lights on so you can see during dusk." He took the controller from her for a moment to turn them on, then gave it back to her. "Just keep a consistent altitude of about forty feet and avoid any trees."

Her eyes held a glint of enthusiasm. "Stay close in case I get into trouble."

"How close do you want me?" he asked.

She took her eyes off the screen just long enough to shoot him a grin. "If you distract me, I might crash. I'm so glad you suggested this. I may have to have a drone of my own."

"It was that most-embarrassing-moment competition that hooked you," he teased.

She laughed. She was no longer the uptight boss lady, and instead was relaxed and smiling. But there was pleasure in her gaze as well.

He went to stand slightly behind her, but to the right so he could see the screen while the drone floated over the empty pastures toward Barn B. She skirted the tree to the left of the structure, slipped around the back side, and followed the side of Barn A to the parking lot. A car sat in the lot. An expensive silver sports car.

"Someone's parked in the lot," Kinley said. She lowered the drone to try and get a glimpse inside. "It looks like it's empty. You don't think someone's trying to break in, do you?"

"Ease around behind the car so we can get the license plate number on the video."

She did as he directed.

"Now go back up and hover over the edge of the roof and follow the roof line."

"You'd better do it." She held the control out to him.

He gripped the edge of the control with his right hand and sandwiched the left stick between his thumb and the side of his hand. He pushed the left stick forward, raising the altitude of the drone to twenty feet, then used the right to move forward over the eve of the barn. He followed the roofline, easing around the side of the structure. The buzzing sound of the propellers had to be loud enough for the person to hear. Where the hell were they?

A man stepped out from beneath the eaves and looked up. Wyatt didn't recognize him. "Do you know him?"

Kinley's tone was hard and her expression tight. "Speak of the devil, and he shall appear. That's my ex."

CHAPTER 11

WYATT STUDIED THE man looking up at the drone. He flashed white teeth that were either caps or he'd spent some time at the dentist having his teeth bleached. His blue dress shirt and dark jeans looked like they'd just been unwrapped from the dry cleaners.

"What's his name?" Wyatt asked.

"Colter Franks."

Jesus. Even his name sounded rich and entitled. Wyatt cocked his head and studied him a moment longer. "He looks like a guy in a toothpaste ad."

Kinley laughed. "You're not too far off. He's a real estate developer."

Colter reached for his cell phone and touched the screen. Kinley's cell phone rang. She ignored it until it went to voice mail. "Ignore him. Maybe he'll get in his car and leave."

"Kinley, now he's seen the drone, the odds of that happening are slim to none."

She blew out a frustrated breath. "Bring the drone home while I deal with him." She jerked the phone up when it rang again. "What do you want, Colter?"

Wyatt turned the drone in the direction of the house, but his attention was focused on the conversation behind him. He couldn't imagine her with someone like Colter Franks. He seemed so completely opposite. What had she seen in him?

"No, there's no reason for you to come here. We don't have anything to discuss."

"No. I have company, and we're going to have dinner."

"No, do not show up at my place of business tomorrow. I have clients all day. I don't have time for you, Colter. I reserve that for the people who deserve it."

Wyatt turned to look over his shoulder at that. Then returned his attention to the drone as it came back in sight. He raised his right hand and captured the drone as he lowered it, then set it on the table, set aside the control, and turned both mechanisms off.

"I told you the last time we spoke that you need to move on with one of the ladies who'll give you what you want. I'm not interested anymore. Please don't call or come to my house or business again."

She pushed the button ending the call.

"Real estate developer," Wyatt repeated her words.

"He dated me because he wants to get his hooks in this property. He was more than a little disappointed when he found out it belongs to my grand-parents instead of me. To protect them when I first started the business, I had them to draw up a lease contract for the land, so the only things I own are the barns and my horse. The land is securely under their control."

"Smart move from an insurance standpoint as well." He nodded. "I guarantee you I'm not interested in your property. As my parents are forever reminding me and my brothers, their ranch will be jointly owned by all three of us one day." What the hell they'd do with it then....

But until then, the only thing he owned were the few personal items he brought with him from San Diego, and his horse Smoke. He had next to nothing to offer her. He'd spent his life fighting terrorists and murderers who terrorized their own country and threatened his. And trying to free people from oppression. And what had that left him with? Not much.

He was developing a fierce desire for the woman in front of him. But what could he offer her other than doing the job she'd hired him to do?

He should never have taken this job. Guaranteed, this job was bound to get in the way of the relationship, or the relationship would get in the way of the job.

He should have figured out something else.

But they'd both been in need. Her of a manager and him of a job away from his parents' ranch.

"If you can shake this off, we can order a meal and enjoy each other's company."

Kinley looped her fingers around his wrist. "It's already shaken. Let's forget the phone ever rang."

Was she really over the guy? Or was she trying hard to be? When she mentioned him before…he'd heard a hint of pain in her voice.

Just how close had they gotten?

Just thinking about that smarmy asshole *with* her….

"Let's check out the barn first to make sure he's gone," he suggested. After dealing with assholes worldwide he didn't trust even the smarmy, toothpaste ad kind. Besides, a drive around in the golf cart would ease her mind and maybe clear his as well.

"I HAVEN'T HAD a Ruben sandwich since I came home for Christmas two years ago." He dipped one last French fry into ketchup and pushed his plate aside. "That was good."

"Where were you last year?" She took a sip of her iced tea they'd switched to.

"Finishing up the paperwork to finalize my separation from the Navy."

So, he hadn't really been in the mood to celebrate. She could understand that. "I was mucking out stalls and feeding horses, just like any other day."

She reached for his hand. Colter's appearance and call had wedged a bit of distance between them. "I have a friend who knows you."

"Who?"

"Her name's Shelley Zimmerman. Shelley Neumann now. She's married. She knows you from high school. She was a freshman when you were a senior."

He gave that some thought. "Five foot nothing with dark hair and a smart mouth"

She chuckled. "That's her. She's not grown much taller since then, and she still has the habit of stating her opinion."

His eyes held a distant look. "She had a crush on my best bud Logan back then."

"So she said."

His expression tightened with emotion. "She was too young, and Logan steered clear. He was working toward a football scholarship and did nothing but train."

"I heard you did the same."

"Yeah, pretty much. My parents could afford to send me, but Logan needed the scholarship, so I trained with him. We both got scholarships."

Something about his face made her wish she hadn't brought it up.

"All that training came in handy when I dropped out of college the second semester of my sophomore year and joined the Navy. Football didn't hold as much appeal to me after Logan was gone. And when I stopped playing, I lost my scholarship. My dad kept saying I needed to finish what I started. Instead I started something new and moved on."

"That wasn't exactly what your dad had in mind, was it?"

"No. But he accepted it…eventually."

And even now he was probably still being the hard-ass who had told his son to move on.

"What do your brothers do for a living?"

"Clay followed in Dad's footsteps and went to law school. He's more into wills, estates, and business law than the criminal aspects. Anthony is an AP Mechanic and works for one of the airlines in San Antonio."

"And you fought terrorists, protected your country, and defended people who couldn't protect themselves." And even though he didn't say it, his father was still disappointed in him.

He got up and began to clear the table. "Five-thirty is going to come quick, I'd better go. We both have a long day tomorrow."

"Leave it, Wyatt, I can do all that."

He dumped his trash in the can and put his dishes in the sink.

The house phone rang, and Kinley glanced at it with a frown. She stepped over to it, but didn't pick it up.

Wyatt studied her expression. "Is it your ex again?"

"No. It's probably just a solicitor."

He glanced at the screen. It read private.

He reached for it, hit the button, and said hello. A distinctive click sounded at the other end. He hung up the phone.

"Is the account in your name, or your grandparents'?"

"My grandparents'."

"It probably was a solicitor targeting older people."

When he led the way to the front door, she followed.

"I enjoyed flying the drone," she said.

"You were a natural."

He turned to face her, reached for the scrunchie holding her hair back and pulled it toward him, releasing her ponytail. Her hair draped over her shoulder, and he ran his fingers through it.

That one slow, sexy action, set her heart to hammering against her ribs.

"I need you to think about something," he said, his voice husky.

"What?"

"You have a habit of taking on strays. Walter, Indira, Tangerine, your therapy patients. Me."

She started to deny that, but he touched her mouth with a fingertip. "You're my boss at work. But to be lovers, we need to be on an equal footing outside the job." He raised his left hand. "This is a permanent part of me. No matter how hard I work to get it back, it will never happen. I've had to accept that." She saw the pain beneath the careful composure of his face. "There's nothing you can do to fix this, either. I'm not one of your patients.

You need to be sure you're getting close to me for the right reasons."

"Wyatt, I've been watching you for days and I haven't seen anything you can't do. Nothing holds you back. You refuse to let this injury define you. Why would you think I'd allow it to define how I see you?"

His tension relaxed. "That was a very good line." He tugged her in against him, cupped the back of her head and took her mouth with a hunger that stole her breath. Their tongues tangled, and every nerve in her body came alive and begged for his touch.

When he raised his head, she dragged his mouth back to hers for a second round.

He broke the kiss to trail his lips to her ear and neck, his breath brushing hot against her skin. When he kissed her again, it was with a tender care that made her knees weak.

His eyes held a tawny heat. "I'd like for you to come out to the cabin for dinner this Saturday." His voice sounded like dark velvet, husky and deep, giving her sensual chills.

"Okay." She ached with need, and when he eased back and put some space between them, she bit back a disappointed sigh. She'd lost her mind. She'd never been like this about a man.

"Ask me to stay, Kinley, and I will."

God, she wanted to. "I can't, not yet."

"Okay." He brushed her lips with another kiss. "I'll see you tomorrow."

It was almost painful when he released her. "Okay." She watched until he got in his car and drove away, then shut and locked the door.

The house phone rang again, dumping ice water over her desire. A tremor shook her. She moved to the phone. The words "private number" appeared on the screen again. If she answered, he'd whisper the same awful things he'd been whispering for the past two weeks. Nausea cramped her stomach and her hands began to shake.

She reached for the electrical plug for the base unit and pulled it out of the wall. The phone instantly stopped ringing. "Fuck you," she whispered at the phone, at the person who was harassing her. She'd call tomorrow and have the landline service canceled. She only left it in place for her grandparents.

But it was hours after she finally went to bed that she closed her eyes and fell asleep.

CHAPTER 12

WYATT SUPERVISED THE morning feeding, then left Gerald in charge of the few riders who came in so he could call Keith Myers for the third time in as many days before things got more hectic.

"I got your messages, Wyatt. Sorry I haven't called you back. What can I do for you?" Keith's voice sounded guarded.

"I'd like to meet with you sometime today. I have something I want to show you."

"I have a full schedule today. Maybe tomorrow."

Keith was blowing him off. Wyatt had suspected it when Keith didn't call him back, but had hoped he'd just been busy. "I have some video of Tangerine. I think you'll find it interesting."

"She's Kinley's problem now, Wyatt."

He remained silent for a moment. "I'm making her my problem too, Keith."

"Good, I'm glad Kinley and Tangerine have you in their corner."

Wyatt ran his hand over his hair. "When did you first start to suspect Hunter Wagner was abusing Tangerine?"

Silence hung over the line for several seconds. "After the jaw injury. She had some other strange injuries before we bred her and I even had the vet out to check her. The vet was suspicious too, but there was nothing definitive. Once she was bred it stopped, then Wagner must have suspected I knew because of the constant supervision I gave him when he came to see her. She was ten months along, and I wasn't taking any chances. That's when he transferred her back to Kinley's."

"Fuck."

"I had no proof, Wyatt." There was an apology in his tone, but also frustration. "To get proof I'd have to let him abuse her. And with her in foal, I couldn't take that chance. Now she's had the foal, maybe you can catch him in the act and report him."

Damnit! "I'm going to do my best."

"Be careful. If he suspects you're onto him, he'll transfer her somewhere else."

"I know. Was it Culver you called?"

"Yeah. He'll remember the call." He was silent a moment. "I really wish I could offer you more. Suspicion was all I had, and the way things were, he could have easily said it was someone on my staff. I couldn't take that chance, so I couldn't turn him in."

"I understand."

"You said you had some video?"

"She's terrified of him. She almost trampled the filly when he came to the stall door."

"So now you have two horses to protect."

"Yeah."

Silence stretched between them. "If there's anything I can do to help you get him...."

At least Keith had balls enough to make the offer. "If I think of anything I'll let you know."

After he hung up, Wyatt paced to shake off the frustration. "Damnit!"

At least Keith was able to protect Tangerine throughout her pregnancy. Now she was no longer gestating, it would be up to them. Wagner would probably find something else to focus his frustrations on until the foal was weaned....

Wyatt shook his head. Someone who would prey on a helpless animal would prey on a human as easily.

They had six months before the foal was weaned. Wagner

wouldn't be able to suspend his need that long. He'd find some kind of substitute. A dog, a cat, another horse he'd stable somewhere else. And there'd be nothing they could do about it because there'd be no way to track it.

"Fuck!"

KINLEY STOOD JUST inside the practice ring. A low-grade tension headache drummed at her temples. She needed to sleep, but couldn't. Since she'd unplugged the land line, someone was using her cell phone number now and calling her at all hours. Because their identity and number were hidden, she couldn't block them. And every time it happened, it frightened her even more.

She'd called her cell phone service provider, but there was nothing they could do to block the caller unless she filed a police report.

It seemed like a no-brainer.

The one thing she had to look forward to that offset the phone calls was Wyatt. He came over every morning and evening to Barn B to check on the boys and make certain they were feeding and caring for the calf.

They'd shared a meal at a restaurant the night before and exchanged more of those hot, thorough, knee weakening kisses he was so good at before he went home. She should have asked him to stay. She'd been more than tempted. And then the phone had rung...

She didn't want to admit to Wyatt that she was being harassed. She needed to deal with it. It wasn't going to stop until she did.

She turned her attention to fifteen-year-old Joshua Mueller who stood ten feet away from her. She wouldn't let what was going on in her life to disrupt her therapy schedule or the care of her patients. She simply needed to push through. Just as she tried to help them to do.

She studied Joshua's expression and tried to judge his mood.

He often swung between anger, self-pity and grief. She'd probably feel the same if she'd been through a life threatening illness.

But the three horses in the ring with him kept their distance because of his attitude. If she could get him to shed some of his anger, she knew they'd go to him. And when they did, he'd learn from their behavior.

Chester, a dun-colored mustang, followed the curve of the railing in search of a blade or two of the grass that grew inside the paddock next to the bottom rail of the fence.

Shawnee, an Appaloosa with a spattering of white spots on her rump, seemed content to look out over the pastures.

Butterfly seemed to be the only one interested in the boy. The paint filly was beautifully marked, with brown shoulders and haunches and a wide, uneven band of white that followed the curve of her belly on each side.

"Remember how we talked about being in the moment last week, Josh?" Kinley asked.

"Yeah, I remember."

"How does your body feel today?" He'd lost the lower part of one leg and the tips of three fingers from septicemia after his brush with bacterial meningitis. But his balance and his posture were both getting better.

His jaw tensed. "My leg hurts. It isn't even there anymore, and it still hurts."

"And your hands?" she asked.

"Not so much. But my handwriting blows."

"Mine does too. That's why I use my computer to type everything. How are you on the computer?"

"I'm okay."

"It wouldn't hurt to ask if you can use your computer to type your homework instead of writing."

His gaze shifted away from her to the open fields and the distant hills beyond. "The others will say something if I get to use one and they don't."

Kinley blinked against the threat of sympathetic tears. "They won't know if you don't tell them. And even if you do, they could start typing their homework too. I'm sure your teachers would be grateful, if their handwriting is as bad as mine." She flashed him a smile.

"I'll ask and see what they say."

She nodded. "Close your eyes," she directed. After he'd closed them, she said, "Now clear your mind and let all that negativity flow out. Breath in through your nose and out through your mouth. In and out. In…and out…

She watched until she saw the tension leave his body. "Now picture the pain in your leg as a baseball and you're going to bat it out of the practice ring. Hear the crack of the bat as it comes in contact with the ball. It's sailing over the fence, then the fields, until it's reaches the hills and disappears into the distance."

For the first time she saw his expression slide into relaxation. Out of the corner of her eye she saw Butterfly moving in a random start and stop toward him. "I don't want you to be startled, but Butterfly is coming to see you, Josh. She's coming up on your left side."

The horse came to a stop parallel to him leaving about three feet between them. Josh remained as he was, eyes closed, his head slightly bowed.

After another pause, Butterfly swished her tail, let out a breath and took two steps closer to him. When she brushed her muzzle along the sleave of his T-shirt, breathing in his scent. Kinley smiled.

Josh slowly raised his head and shifted to look at Butterfly. They seemed to gaze at one another for a at least a minute. When he raised a hand and stroked the horse's jaw, Kinley found herself grinning. He turned toward Butterfly, and she took a step closer to curve her muzzle over his shoulder in a kind of hug. Josh leaned his head against her neck and rested his right hand against her broad, muscular chest.

They stayed in that position for several moments, until Butterfly shifted. Josh straightened and ran a hand down her neck. He murmured something to her that Kinley couldn't hear and stepped back. After a brief pause, Butterfly wandered away across the practice ring.

Josh turned aside to dry his tear-wet face on the tail of his T-shirt. "Why did she do that?"

"Horses are sensitive to emotions, Josh. They can sense anger and aggression, pain and sadness. When you released your tension and anger, it allowed her an opening to approach you and offer comfort.

"People can't sense emotion as keenly as horses can, but much like horses, anger and aggression drive them away. When you're calm and open to being approached, it draws them in.

"Why don't we walk the circle and see who else might want to come to you?"

He nodded.

By the end of their session, Kinley felt emotionally drained. She tried to maintain a distance from the clients, but Josh's emotional struggles with the amputation of his leg, the continuing pain he experienced, and the adjustment he was working through because of the missing first joint of three of his fingers, were hard to ignore.

But two of the three horses had come to him. She'd promised in a few more weeks she'd get him up in the saddle and teach him to ride. But he needed to show her he could maintain control of his runaway temper and develop some patience. By the time he'd done that, his balance issues would be much better as well.

She called Diane to report how well today went.

"Don't be surprised or get discouraged if the next time he comes he's worked up again. It comes and goes depending on what kind of day or week they have at home or at school."

Kinley didn't want to let her high slip away just yet. "I wish you could have seen how Butterfly responded to him, and how much calmer he was once they connected."

"I wish I could have too. He's making progress with me, too. He's going to get through this and be fine. He's a strong kid."

"Yes, he is." He had to be to have survived the illness and related surgeries he went through. "I'll send you my notes on the session as soon as I type them up."

"Thanks."

She ended the call and went back to her office. She'd just settled behind her desk when Wyatt came to the door. Her heart leapt at sight of him. "Hey," she greeted him and beckoned for him to come in. "Everything all right?"

"Yeah, everything's fine." He closed the door and came further into the room.

She reached for a note she'd written. "I have a guy coming to give me an estimate on a security system for the barns. He'll be here around two tomorrow." She offered him the note.

Wyatt tucked the note into his jeans pocket. "I'll wander around with him and make sure he understands what you want."

"Thanks."

"Are you free for dinner tonight after work?" he asked.

Her sleepless nights had to be showing. "Yes."

"I thought we could go out to the ranch and I'll throw something on the grill. How's seven for you?"

"Sounds good. It'll give me time to run home and shower off the horse."

He grinned. "Will you come out from behind the desk for a minute?"

Curious, she rose and walked around to him.

He bent his head and brushed his lips across her cheek. "I don't smell anything but you." he said close to her ear, sending delightful shivers through her. He tugged her close and kissed her. He took his time, tempting, teasing, his tongue titillatingly thorough. She hummed beneath the pressure of the kiss and gripped the back of his shirt in both fists, holding him tight. When he raised his head, she was breathless and aching with need.

"I'll see you later. After work." He brushed one more kiss across her lips. His thumb lingered against her cheek. "Are you sure you're okay?"

"Yes, I'm fine." If he could get her this worked up with a kiss, she'd be toast if he did anything else.

CHAPTER 13

WYATT TUGGED A knife free of the wooden block, centered the freshly rinsed asparagus on the cutting board and, holding the heel of his weak hand against the bundle to keep it in place, sawed off the bottom inch of the stalks. He lay the bundle on a sheet of aluminum foil and spread it out to sprinkle with salt and pepper, added a couple of pats of butter, a dash of Italian seasoning on top for good measure, and then wrapped the edges tight.

Packets of chicken breasts smothered in onions and green peppers had already gone on the grill while he slid a covered casserole dish of rice into the oven and set the timer.

"You never told me you can cook," Kinley said as she watched from her seat at the end of kitchen island.

"When you live alone and there's no one else to cook, your survival instincts kick in and you learn to grill."

Kinley laughed. By the time he picked her up at her house, she'd showered and changed into red shorts to show off her long, shapely legs, well-muscled from riding, and a short-sleeved, scoop neck pullover with bright flowers of the same color.

Kinley brushed her ponytail back over her shoulder and leaned forward on folded arms to watch him work. She seemed unaware that she flashed just a hint of cleavage.

He tried to keep his mind on getting the meal prepared instead of what he'd really like to be doing. "If you do it right, there's no dishes to wash. Everything goes into the refrigerator, trash, or the dishwasher, and you're done."

"I'm going to take notes."

He'd uncorked one of the bottles of white wine he brought with him from California. Deciding it had breathed long enough, he paused to pour her a glass and set it in front of her.

Up close the honey tones of her hair were sun streaked liberally with a paler hue, almost white. She'd tied it back at the base of her neck with a black ribbon and the heavy length of it hung down her back in waves and spirals. Before the end of the night he'd have it freed so he could explore its texture.

"So, you don't cook?" he asked.

"I do, but I'm one of those kitchen nightmares who uses every pot and pan in the place to fix one dish. It's a skill passed down from my mom and grandmother."

He chuckled. "My mom's become the crockpot wonder. I think she might even fix bacon and eggs in the crockpot. I know she bakes cakes in one now and then. We're having one of her creations for dessert. It's some kind of chocolate cake with cherry pie filling poured over it. I have whipped cream to put on top. She left the can."

"That's some hard-core slow cooker skills. You two need to get together and trade secrets."

The oven timer went off, and he went to check the rice, stirred it, and reset the timer for ten more minutes.

"I'll put this on the grill with the chicken, then jump in the shower. If you don't mind."

"No, go do what you need to do." She waved a hand toward the hallway. "I'll just snoop through everything in here and find out all your secrets."

All his personal stuff was still in storage. "Good luck."

He put the asparagus on the grill, closed the lid and went back inside. He was in and out of the shower in five minutes. He stared at his image in the steamed-up mirror while he dragged on underwear one-handed. The cramps in his hand were getting worse. He was going to have to see one of the specialists. How the hell did his fingers hurt when the rest of his hand felt numb? It made no sense. But he'd think about that later. Right now he just wanted to enjoy being with Kinley.

He dragged on his usual cargo shorts and T-shirt, ran a comb through his hair, noticed that he needed a haircut, and stuck his feet into beige canvas deck shoes that had seen better days. He went into the living room, noticed Kinley was nowhere in sight, checked the rice and, seeing it was done, turned off the timer and the oven.

Outside he found Kinley relaxing on the porch in one of the Adirondack chairs. The remnants of tension he noticed when he picked her up had finally relaxed.

"This is a beautiful place," she said softly.

"Yeah, it is, but I'm thinking about getting an apartment closer to work."

"Why?"

"I'd better check the chicken." He went down the steps to a section of the carport he'd made into his grilling area with his gas grill and a small table and a caddy holding tongs, forks, and spatulas.

Finding the chicken and asparagus done, he plucked the foil packets off the grill with tongs and set them on a platter. He turned the grill off and, gripping the platter with his good hand and bracing his weak arm under it for extra support, he carried the food back up on the porch.

Kinley wiggled out of the chair to get the door.

"It's a thirty-minute drive to and from work," he said as he entered the house and set the platter on the kitchen table. And as long as he was here, his mother would continue to snoop.

"Thirty minutes is nothing compared to that view," Kinley said turning to look out the door at the distant hills.

It was the view he remembered first when he thought of home. What did that say about him and his parents? "As kids until we graduated high school, we practically lived down here in this cabin. I think my mom liked us being down here because we weren't wrecking our rooms or tracking mud into the house.

"Back then it wasn't quite as updated as it is now, but it allowed us to stretch our wings and be independent. She insisted that we go up to the house to eat dinner every night, though." He went to a cabinet to get out plates and silverware while Kinley got paper towels and folded them into napkins to finish setting the table.

Without being asked, Kinley grabbed potholders, got the round casserole dish of rice out of the oven, and set it in the center of the platter.

"Then why move?" she asked again.

"Because my mother is a snoop. She'd eased off a bit for a couple of weeks, but she seems to think I need to be checked on every day. She makes excuses for coming by."

Her brows rose. "The dessert?"

"Yeah."

"Maybe it's just the only way she feels she can mother you. My grandmother always says I look like I've lost weight every time they come in for a visit. Even though I've been the same size forever."

He held her seat for her until she sat down, and then he retrieved her wine glass from the island and refilled it.

"Did you do something to make her think you need to be checked on?" she asked.

He opened a packet of chicken and vegetables and set it beside her plate. "I'm different from the man they thought they were raising. I didn't get a college degree and a job. I enlisted in the Navy and moved to California. My brothers are successful in their fields, come to visit every couple of months, and have families. They can relate to them. They can't relate to me."

"Some of that is my fault. In the last ten years I've spent as much time out of the country as in it. Gone places and done things I couldn't share with them even if I wanted to. During those times I'd be out of touch, sometimes for weeks at a time. They love me because I'm their son, but not because they know me."

Her expression shifted, and he wondered if he'd put her off

by being too blunt.

He rose to get a drink. He returned to the table with two bottles of iced tea. He changed the subject. "Did you grow up around here?"

"No, San Antonio. After I graduated from college I moved in with my grandparents, and you already know the rest."

"What about your parents and siblings?"

"My parents travel. They don't really have a home base. The longest they've settled anywhere is six months" She spooned some rice onto her plate. "I'm an only child."

He wasn't surprised. She'd never mentioned any siblings.

"Any cousins?"

"Sure, on my dad's side. A couple, but we're not close."

"I can't imagine growing up without my brothers. We played sports together, had swimming tournaments in the pool up at the house, fought, fished, camped out, rode everything on four legs and four or two wheels."

"And then after they left for college you were here alone?"

"No. Logan and I moved in here together our senior year. He always hung out with my brothers, too. We had a gym set up in one of the bedrooms and we worked out and studied our asses off."

"So your parents trusted you to get up each morning and get yourself to school?" Her brows rose.

"That was the deal. If we didn't keep the place clean or we missed school, even one day, we had to both move back in with our parents. I was already working here on the ranch during the summer, and afternoons after school and weekends, so it wasn't really a hardship. Logan had summer jobs and weekend stuff to do too. We were used to getting up early."

"You never really got to be a kid, Wyatt."

He took a swallow of tea and shrugged. "It prepared me for college and for BUD/s when I joined the Navy."

"They pretty much cut you loose when you were seventeen, Wyatt." She sounded outraged.

Wyatt grinned. "Hey, we were better prepared for college than ninety percent of the student body. Mom was down here all the time checking on us, feeding us. And Logan's mom did the same. We had as much parental support as we wanted."

She shook her head. "There's a fine balance. I had too much supervision. I was an only child, so my parents monitored every class I took, every person I came into contact with, and every extra-curricular activity I participated in. They vetted my teachers, and my friends. My only freedom was to come to my grandparents on holidays and summers, so my parents could have—" She made quotation marks with her fingers—"'time to themselves.' By the time I graduated, I couldn't wait to leave home. And they couldn't wait to sell their house and start traveling."

He paused in mid-bite. "They sold your home and just left?"

"Yes. But I had my grandparents to depend on. My Dad can work remotely from anywhere. He's a financial analyst for several big corporations. And my mom's an expert in squeezing every dime and nickel he earns. They call now and then, but they're more interested in each other than they are me or my grandparents."

And then her grandparents left to retire in Florida, leaving her alone again. It seemed he and Kinley had more in common than they realized.

THEY LINGERED OVER desert. Wyatt held out his hand and said, "Let's go for a walk. I'll show you around the property and introduce you to Smoke."

A strong breeze tugged at Kinley's hair and she twisted it into a rope and tossed it over her shoulder. Wyatt Laced his fingers with hers and matched her shorter stride as they followed a well-worn path toward the stables.

The sound of distant lowing reached them as they approached the barn. Cattle dotted the green stretch of pasture that stretched to the distant hills. The ranch was bigger than her own. The barn was huge, and she suddenly realized it was actually two barns. One for livestock and the other for machinery with a bunkhouse farther down.

"We're having a barbecue with my brothers and their families in a few weeks at Mom and Dad's house. I'd like for you to come." She noticed he didn't refer to the house as home. It was "Mom and Dad's." He always referred to the ranch as his dad's, too.

If she attended, his family might assume there was more to Wyatt's relationship with her than what was truly there. But if she didn't go, she felt he wouldn't have anyone in his corner. She realized that, for all his strength, Wyatt triggered some protective instinct in her, as much as she did the same in him. She looked up to find him watching her. "I'd love to come."

He nodded, a quick smile flitting across his face and he leaned down to brush her lips with a kiss. "Good."

He tugged the barn door open and flipped on the lights. Equine heads poked out of each stall, and at the end of the aisle, one horse whinnied.

Wyatt offered a rub here and a pat there, going down the line of horses until he reached the end. In the last stall a solid black head remained. The horse's mane lay thick against one side of his neck, and his dark, liquid eyes focused on Wyatt. He whinnied again and stomped his feet. "I'm coming," Wyatt replied with a chuckle. "Hey." He placed his hands on either side of the horse's jaw and rested his forehead against his in greeting, then drew back. "We didn't get to ride today, but we will tomorrow. How's that?"

The horse blew out a breath with a snort.

Kinley laughed. "I don't think he believes you."

"It's been a couple of days." He removed a lead hung on the wall and stepped aside to open the stall door, then hooked the lead to Smoke's halter. The big horse, at least sixteen hands, practically pranced out of the stall. "You could show the lady how handsome you are and smile, Smoke."

Smoke drew his lips back and bared his teeth in a horsey grin.

Kinley laughed. "He's beautiful. Does he have Friesian in his lineage?"

"And quarter horse."

Smoke seemed to give her the once-over, then approached her. Kinley extended a hand and he tilted his big head into her palm like a cat. "He's wonderful."

"And he knows it," Wyatt said affectionately as he patted Smoke's sleek, dark side. "He's been my only constant here. No matter how long I'm away, or what I'm dealing with, he always greets me like he's been waiting for me."

"That's the way Silver was with me. They don't forget you. And I believe they have the ability to love."

"Maybe so." He paused in thought. "We had a War Dog in our platoon. A Belgian Malinois. Jones, the teammate who handled him, left the unit, and you could tell the dog grieved over his absence. We'd be waiting for men to get off planes or helicopters, and he'd be looking at each one as they deplaned, like he was looking for someone in particular. When they retired the dog, our team leader contacted Jones to let him know.

The day the adoption paperwork went through and Jones came to pick up the dog, we all went down to give him one last pat and send him on his way. He'd been an excellent teammate, saved our asses numerous times. The dog went crazy as soon as he saw Jones, like he'd found his long, lost brother."

Kinley struggled to maintain her composure. "I'm glad he got to go home with the special someone he'd bonded with."

Wyatt nodded. "When I move off the ranch, I want to take Smoke with me. I've left him behind too many times already."

She cut him off. "We have an empty stall in Barn B. You'll want your own mount to ride the trails and fence lines."

"I wasn't hinting, Kinley."

She shrugged, "One of the perks to the job."

"Give the lady a thank-you kiss, Smoke."

The big horse turned his muzzle to carefully mouth her cheek. Kinley stroked his neck in response. "You're a sweet boy, aren't you?"

Smoke nodded. Kinley laughed. If Wyatt could teach his horse to do all that, she'd chosen the right man to deal with the horses and the boarding barn. Her last little bit of reserve fell away.

When Wyatt linked his fingers with hers as they walked back to the cabin, she realized how much she'd already begun to depend on him. But was it fair for her to dump personal stuff on him too?

Was the caller Colter? Or had Hunter Wagner somehow figured out they suspected him of injuring Tangerine? It had to be Colter. But the calls started almost two weeks before he came back around. And it seemed out of character for him. He used charm to get what he wanted, not threats.

CHAPTER 14

IT TOOK ONLY minutes to clean up after the meal. "More wine, Kinley?" Wyatt asked as he tossed the last of the foil debris into the trash.

"No. Just some water please." She wandered to the couch and sat down.

Wyatt got two bottles of cold water out of the fridge, and took a seat next to her, but didn't crowd her. "You can prop your feet up on the coffee table and relax if you like."

"Did you ever get in touch with Myers?" she asked.

He'd hoped to go one evening without talking about business. "Yeah. He told me he had Doc Culver out to check Tangerine for injuries twice while they had her. He as much as admitted that he suspected Hunter Wagner of abusing her. He and his staff kept careful check on her the remainder of the time they had her at their barn. But he couldn't catch Wagner in the act because he never gave him an opportunity to be alone with her. He couldn't take the chance and risk the foal. Then Wagner moved her to your barn."

She tilted her head back and seemed to study the big, wooden beams, thick as railroad ties, that crossed the living room. "I've been getting harassing phone calls late at night for the past three weeks. First it was on the house phone. When I unplugged that, he started calling my cell."

"What does he say when you answer?"

"He calls me a bitch or…other things. It started before Colter called me. I don't think it's him."

"His call the other night would be a coincidence, then?" Wyatt commented. "He seemed insistent on seeing you."

"He said he had something important to discuss with me, but the only thing important to him is real estate, so I can't think what he wants."

"Maybe he was priming the well. Get you frightened about staying alone at the house and then swoop in to save the day."

"Colter?" She laughed. "Not very likely. One day a rattlesnake decided to sun himself on my deck, Colter screamed when he saw it. The snake was not impressed."

And from the tone of her voice, neither was she.

"I went in and got my Kimber, shot it, and killed it."

He offered his fist to bump and she smiled and bumped it with hers.

After a moment's thought he said, "Maybe you should call him and find out why he wants to talk to you. You can record the conversation and compare the two voices."

"It doesn't sound like Colter. But it's someone whispering, so it's hard to tell."

Had Wagner decided to yank Kinley's chain because she hired him? But he'd acted like he didn't know she had until recently.

"I believe it's a man because of the aggression in his tone," she added.

Her mentioning aggression in the interaction jacked his pulse up a notch and his concern. "When exactly did the calls start?"

"A week before you were hired."

"How many days after the filly was born?"

"Five days. It was the same day I got your background check back, and the same day Shelley came to tell me she was pregnant. The bastard called right after she left and called me a bitch."

He might have been watching when Shelley left. Damnit! "I've been working with you for almost a month, Kinley. Why didn't you tell me?"

"I've been solving my own issues since long before you showed up, Wyatt. I'm used to dealing with things on my own."

"You haven't filed a police report. Why not?"

"I unplugged the house phone and thought it would stop once he couldn't call that number. But then he started calling my cell phone. Which makes sense, since that's the number associated with the business, and everyone has access to it. I tried to block him, but you have to know the number he's calling from to do that."

"So that leaves a police report and signing over permission for them to trace the numbers when he calls."

"He doesn't stay on the line long enough for that. He just whispers insults and then hangs up."

"The police can get the number as it comes in, Kinley, and trace it back to the phone it's coming from."

"He doesn't have to stay on the line?"

"No." He shook his head. "I went after the doctor who screwed up my arm, through the courts, both the military and the San Diego County courts. The military kicked him to the curb with a less-than-honorable, not because he screwed up the surgery, but because he lied about it and tried to use the police in San Diego as his personal stalkers to intimidate me into dropping the whole thing."

"He called in wellness checks every day for two months. Called in false reports saying I was stalking him when I was sitting in my apartment or at the gym. I installed cameras in my apartment and outside it to record the police visits, and used my phone to record my every move. It wasn't until I showed the police where I was, and provided witnesses, that they started to investigate him instead of me." He unclenched his fists. "It quickly became obvious what he was doing, and the police started documenting the numbers the calls came from and where the cell phones pinged from.

They finally put a team in the parking lot of my apartment and caught him parked outside, calling them to report that I needed a wellness check, and arrested him for calling in a false report. They were able to trace the prepaid phones to several stores along his route home and got videos of him purchasing them. He was charged with harassment by the District Attorney in San Diego, and because there was so much evidence against him, he was offered a plea deal. A year in jail.

The DA shared the evidence with the criminal division, and they decided to fast-track the court martial, I think the DA decided he'd save the county money and let a military court dish out more punishment.

"The military cut him loose, but because the DA downgraded the charges to harassment instead of stalking, no one took away his license to practice medicine or checked any of the other cases he handled while he was enlisted. He's already out of jail after six months for good behavior and stepped right back into a medical practice.

"The doctors tried to put me on meds for my anger issues, but I refused them. They pushed through my medical discharge as quickly as they could so I'd just go away and shut up."

"I have a malpractice suit filed against him, but it may be years before it's settled. It isn't about the money. It's about the bastard fucking up and trying to hide it. And him going off the reservation to try and get me thrown in jail and court-martialed. He'd have destroyed my reputation in the teams, cost me my benefits, and gone on his merry way like nothing had happened.

"So I did it to him instead. Or I guess you could say he did it to himself."

He rested an arm on the back of the couch behind her as he turned to her. "Don't let this asshole screw with you, Kinley. A few phone calls don't sound like much, but it can escalate into more. File the report so there's a record. I'll go with you if you want me to."

"You don't have to. I'll file it tomorrow."

He didn't realize how tense he was until she spoke. "Good."

She moved in close against him and curled against his side.

He looped his bad arm around her.

"I'm sorry you had to go through all that." She ran a soothing hand back and forth across his T-shirt-covered chest.

Heat trailed down his torso to his groin and he hardened in an instant. "I'm okay, Kinley." The words tasted like a lie, but all he could think was how good her hand felt while it caressed his chest, and what it would feel like if it moved lower. The scent of her vanilla shampoo lingered in her hair. He breathed it in.

When she moved to look up at him, he cupped her chin and kissed her. Kinley broke the kiss to straddle his lap and he nearly groaned when her mouth came back to his. It had been too long.

With his hands beneath her shirt, he followed the lean contours of her body and unhooked her bra. He couldn't feel with his left hand, but was careful to maintain a light pressure against her skin. With his right he discovered what he'd already observed. She was slender and strong, her skin soft. But he hadn't expected how beautiful her breasts would be. He cupped the weight of one and brushed his thumb over her nipple until it beaded.

"You're moving awfully slow, cowboy," she said, her breath warm against his ear.

She nibbled at his neck, and a fresh flood of blood rushed south.

"I want to be thorough. Every mission is about the details." He had a desire to pamper her, since she never pampered herself. But he was working with one hand tied behind his back. His clumsy left hand wouldn't do what he wanted unless he was watching it. Muscle memory just didn't work when you couldn't feel things.

But there wasn't a damn thing wrong with the rest of him. His rock-hard erection and aching balls could attest to that.

She cupped his face in her hands and kissed him again. "What mission are you on right now?"

"To please you." And to end his long, lo-o-ong dry spell without sex.

Her eyes went dark and she smiled. "Good answer."

He lifted the hem of her blouse, and she raised her arms to slip out of it, then leaned forward and did that shrug and wiggle all women seemed to know, and shucked her bra. The way she did it seemed sexier than every woman he'd ever been with before. Her breasts, round and full, were eye level with him. The pale peach nipples tipped up at him, begging to be tasted, and he clasped her waist to bring her in closer so he could reach one nipple with his mouth, and feathered the underside with his tongue, then sucked. He couldn't touch her enough, hold her enough. For once he forgot about his numb hand and just touched her.

When he turned to capture the other nipple and suck, Kinley hummed with pleasure, ran her fingers through his hair and caressed the back of his neck. He tilted his head back to look up at her and she kissed him again. He urged her to her feet. "Second door on the left."

Once in his room, Kinley jerked his T-shirt up, and he raised his arms to help. She kicked off her shoes and wiggled out of her shorts while he dropped his cargo shorts.

He'd never have guessed that she'd wear a thong. He'd never seen anything as sexy as Kinley dressed in nothing but that tiny scrap of lace and the thin band of elastic holding it in place. Her body was sleek and lightly muscled, and her breasts were full, with those pale peach nipples waiting for more attention.

He caught the end of the ribbon she'd tied her hair back with and tugged until it pulled away, then draped her hair over her shoulder. "I've wanted to see your hair free, Kinley."

Color flooded her cheeks, her eyes darkened, and she bit her bottom lip. When she would have looped her thumbs in the elastic and removed her thong, Wyatt caught her hand and said, "Let me."

Kinley slid back on the bed. When he dropped his boxer briefs and stepped out of them, her gaze snagged on his erection, and he went painfully hard. He crawled up the bed to her and eased her thong down each leg, slowly dragging it out, and dropped it over the edge of the bed.

He poised above her, letting her feel his body align with hers, skin to skin, as he kissed her. Kinley ran her hands up his back, and her hips rose to meet him as he eased inside her. The warm-wet grip of her body nearly ripped his control away. It had been too long for him. Need took over and he thrust deep.

Kinley came to the realization she'd always thought of sex as a straightforward, body-meets-body-and-finds-pleasure kind of situation. She'd been entertained, coaxed, and teased into orgasm during sex, but never seduced.

Wyatt Taylor seduced her. With every intent, heated look in his gold-tinted eyes, every brush of his lips and tongue, every caress, and every movement of his body against hers, he seduced her. He pulled the ribbon from her hair, and slid her thong down her legs, like he was unwrapping a gift he'd waited for a long time. For her it was the icing on the seduction cake. She'd never been so turned on.

And now, with every thrust he drove every nerve inside her into a frenzy of tormenting pleasure that built and crested into an overwhelming orgasm. For the first time in her life, she cried out because she couldn't control it. She'd barely started to recover, when he began to move again. The same sweet, frenetic thrill took over, and she reached for it again, opening herself to him, meeting him with every thrust. The pulse of his release inside her triggered another orgasm nearly as powerful as the first.

After several moments, Wyatt moved to lie beside her and cuddle her against his side. A lazy smile curved his lips. "Am I a good fit?"

She laughed. "Oh, God. I was hoping you'd forget that."

His sexy mouth spread into a grin that made her want to kiss him again. "Not a chance."

"I knew it was going to come back to haunt me."

He chuckled and gave her waist a squeeze. "Even though I gave you my application, I was semi-hoping you wouldn't hire me. I was worried about how I'd manage to keep my distance."

She thought she'd done a fine job maintaining a professional distance, but all she'd been doing was hiding. "I tried to stay away the first couple of weeks."

"I noticed."

"You needed time to be the boss and teach the hands to think of you that way. You probably had that down the first day."

"The people who work for you already recognized you needed help, Kinley, so that gave them a reason to accept me."

"Maybe at first, but now they accept you because you've earned their trust. You know what you're doing, and you know how to handle things when the unexpected happens." She caressed his chest, enjoying the muscular feel of him and the light scattering of hair there.

The dull sound of knocking came from somewhere.

Wyatt raised his head. "Someone's at the front door. I'll be right back." He eased his arm from around her, brushed her lips with a kiss, and rolled off the bed. He grabbed his cargo shorts off the floor, tugged them on, and in the process, gave her a very nice view of his bare behind and his broad back. He grabbed his T-shirt as he strode out of the bedroom.

Wyatt tugged the shirt on raked the fingers of his right hand through his hair and opened the front door. His mother stood on the porch. "Hey, Mom." He stepped out onto the porch and closed the door behind him. "What's going on?"

"I wanted to let you know there's a line of bad thunderstorms coming through the area. I saw you had company and thought you might want to get her home before they hit."

Wyatt kept his expression blank with an effort. "Why didn't you just call my cell phone?"

"I just came over from the stables. I went by to check on Rosie, and didn't have my cell with me. She gets a little anxious when it storms, so I put a pressure blanket on her to soothe her. Since she's lost her sight, she's hyper-sensitive to loud noises."

The defensive emotions coursing through him settled. The old mare had been with his mom for twenty-eight years. And even though Rosie had lost her sight, his mother still took the old horse out on walks more than on rides close to the house.

"You should have called me. I could have gone over and done that for you. I'll notify Kinley about the storms. We may need to check the horses. We have one who just foaled four weeks ago, and she's high-strung."

"That might be a good idea." Lightning flashed in the distance, and thunder soon followed. "I'm going back up to the house before the waterworks start. You may want to try a pressure blanket on the new mother, too. It sure soothes Rosie."

"Thanks, Mom." He watched her climb the concrete steps up the hill until she reached the top. Wyatt swore beneath his breath. No wonder Kinley didn't have a life outside of work.

Kinley's blouse and bra, tossed over the arm of the couch, triggered a grin as he scooped them up to take them to her.

In the bedroom she lay curled on her side, the spread tugged over her. When he ran a finger along her forearm, she opened her eyes and smiled. "Is everything okay?"

"Yeah. Mom came down to put a pressure blanket on one of the older horses. A series of storms are headed our way, and lightning's already flashing in the distance. It'll hit here in about fifteen minutes. Are any of the horses other than Tangerine likely to get worked up?"

She frowned in thought and brushed a long strand of hair back off her cheek. "None in Barn B. Arrow might get a little pissy. I usually check on them several times during storms."

He eased in beside her and ran his hand under the bedspread to stroke the bare skin of her hip. "I wanted you to spend the night."

"I would have liked that. But you can pack a bag and spend the night at my house after we've checked the horses."

He hoped she'd say that. "I have a go bag in the car."

She raised her brows in surprise.

"It's just something we did in the Navy. I keep a change at the office, too."

"Wise man." She threaded her fingers through his hair and brushed it back from his forehead. "I have to get dressed."

He grinned. "I wish you didn't, but—"

She sat up and let the bedspread fall to her waist. "Kiss me first."

He wondered if it was really thunder he heard rumbling outside, or the sound of his own heartbeat in his ears when all the blood rushed out of his head and back into his dick. Jesus, he'd wanted women before, but not like this. He kissed her, and was rewarded as her tongue tangled with his and she reached for him.

Thunder crashed so close it rattled the windows, and they broke apart. Wyatt got up to change clothes. reached for her thong, and handed it to her. "You don't wear anything like that to work, do you?" he asked as he got clean jeans from the closet and a shirt.

She flashed him a grin. "You'll have to find out sometime."

CHAPTER 15

RAIN HAMMERED THE windshield like the clouds were buckets being emptied right over the car. The windshield wipers were set on high, but the brief visibility they created did little good. Despite the deluge and the huge gusts of wind buffeting the car, Wyatt seemed relaxed but focused. On the other hand, every muscle in her body was tight with anxiety.

"It's been a while since it's rained like this," she commented. Kinley tugged the jacket Wyatt gave her to wear tighter around her. Even after she folded the sleeves, it still swallowed her.

"This is a drizzle compared to the rainy seasons in South America and Africa." He glanced in her direction then back straight ahead. "At one point in Africa I had to hang my head out the window to see the road, and it was a dirt track. Then there were the ruts where the jeep would get stuck and we'd have to bail out and push it, then pile back in to drive two or three hundred feet and do it all over again. This is a walk in the park."

She tried to find comfort in knowing he had experience driving in challenging conditions. But she couldn't shake her worries about Tangerine and the baby. The mare was so traumatized and the baby was in the stall with her. If the storm settled over the farm for long, she might react badly and accidentally trample the filly. They were running just ahead of the lightning and accompanying thunder, so maybe they'd get there in time to move the filly to another stall until the front moved on.

At a time like this, Shelley would be telling her she couldn't be responsible for every second of every day and night at the barns. She provided a safe stall, a well-grounded structure, food, grooming, and care. She couldn't control everything.

And she didn't regret taking the evening for her and Wyatt. She'd been so fixated on making the stables pay for themselves, and making a profit, she'd lost track of having any kind of personal life. That was probably why she dated Colter. It had been so long since she was able to enjoy any male attention. Thank God she'd recognized what was happening before she slept with him. Come to think of it, she hadn't been all that keen on sleeping with him, which made it easier to come up with excuses not to. This night with Wyatt had done a lot to soothe her bruised confidence.

Wyatt turned right on the main road and traffic picked up. He kept his distance from the car ahead of him. At one red light the SUV hydroplaned because of the water standing on the road. Kinley found herself pushing on the floor like she was in control of the brakes and braced a hand on the door. Wyatt regained control of the vehicle with no issue and came to a stop with room to spare. Five minutes later the rain eased back to a lighter drizzle, and she whooshed out a breath in relief.

When they reached the barn she said, "I'll go with you in case you need help with Tangerine and the baby. Then let's go over and check my barn."

"Okay." He parked as close to the door as possible, and they both bailed out of the car and dashed to the door to stand under the awning.

Wyatt punched in the numbers on the electronic lock, opened the door, and stepped aside for her to go in first.

Everything seemed quiet. All the horses but one came to look out of their stall.

Wyatt walked down to look into Tangerine's stall, then gave her a thumbs-up that all was well.

A crack of thunder sounded like a gunshot, and Kinley jerked in response. Two of the horses lunged back from their stall doors and she went to check on them. One moved back against the side wall, but calmed. The other went to the hay rack and started nibbling. She strode on down the barn and paused to take a look at Tangerine.

The mare seemed unperturbed by the thunder, but she remained in her favorite corner with the filly.

"She doesn't seem to be afraid of the noise. I think we're in the clear here," Wyatt said as she joined him. "I'll check the rest.

She watched the mare with her baby while he did the check. One person breaking faith with a horse could damage them for life. A dog could be abused and come right back, hoping for love, but horses were different creatures. It took years to get the animal to rebuild a relationship with any human after they'd been mistreated. Wagner had done more damage than he'd ever understand. And he obviously didn't care.

She left the mare and strode down to where Wyatt stood at the back door. "Why don't you stay here while I check the other barn," he said.

"Arrow is over there. He might be upset."

"If he is, you need to stay out of the way, Kinley. He was hard to handle with me and Gerald both on him. We'll make sure he's confined and unable to harm himself."

"I've dealt with him before. Maybe he'll respond to me."

"Even with this, we're both going to get drenched," he warned and opened the large umbrella he'd collected from the office.

With his arm around her, they dashed out of the back door and into the deluge, then ran around the practice circle to the other barn. They'd barely reached the awning over the door when lightning zig-zagged across the sky like it hoped to rip the heavens open. Thunder followed almost instantly with a sonic boom and a crackle.

Kinley grabbed Wyatt's arm and pulled him in closer to the door. "Nothing's worth getting struck by lightning." He slipped an arm around her, and she leaned against him, borrowing his heat. The shorts that seemed such a good idea before left her legs vulnerable in the rain-chilled air. She shivered while Wyatt keyed in the code, opened the door, and ushered her inside. A high-pitched whinny came from one of the back stalls. It sounded like Arrow was being his usual pissy self.

"I seem to remember a throw on the back of the couch in your office. You can warm up while I check on all of them."

"I'm okay. I'll warm up after we're through." She went down one side of the barn while Wyatt took the other.

They both ended up at Arrow's stall. The stallion paced restlessly back and forth in the stall and kicked at the back wall. "He's a pain in the ass," Wyatt commented.

Kinley laughed. "Yes, he is. If he gets any more worked up, I have some medication to help calm him down. I'll have to call his owner before I give it to him, though."

The horse kicked the wall again and Wyatt raised a brow. "Make the call just in case."

WYATT LOOKED OVER the pasture closest to the barn. Boggy patches with standing water in them dotted the green surface here and there, but he didn't see any damage. The phones had been hot all day with clients calling to check on their animals.

Finally he needed a break, and asked Carol to take over for him while he did some cleanup around the parking lot. He drove Kinley's golf cart into the parking lot and parked beneath the big Texas ash tree. He got the chainsaw and, laying it on the ground, started to brace a foot on it, then looked at his left arm and hand in disgust. He'd never be able to control the saw with his left hand. He texted Kyle, one of the part-time workers, to come help him. The young man came sauntering out of Barn B and wandered down the hill.

"How are you with a chainsaw?" Wyatt asked as soon as Kyle reached him.

"When I was teething, I had a chew toy that was a chainsaw. I've been clearing trees every winter since."

Wyatt laughed. "Okay. I need you to cut up this limb and take the wood to Kinley's house. She has a woodpile in back for the fireplace."

Kyle, with easy skill, made quick work of the large limb, and they loaded the fireplace-sized chunks onto the trailer hooked to the back of the cart. Several smaller limbs lay scattered beneath it, and they loaded those as well. "Dump those smaller limbs at the compost center behind the storage shed behind Barn B. We'll run them through the shredder to use for bedding."

"Will do."

Resigned to going back to his office, he was relieved when a van pulled into the lot with the name of a security company on the side and a man got out. Wyatt introduced himself and found out the man was from the company Kinley called.

"The cameras you have…?" he asked.

"The storm knocked the ones in Barn B out, but I haven't had time to get them back up this morning. I'll take care of that until Ms. Green decides on what she wants installed. In the meantime, let's walk around, and I'll show you what she has in mind."

Less than half an hour later, Wyatt left the technician writing up his estimate to deal with the arrival of the farrier.

The technician returned with an itemized list of all the security cameras and alarms they could want on their dream list, plus a more reasonable list of the ones he thought they really needed. The cost for both was more than he thought Kinley could afford to spend. He'd have to walk over and discuss it with her. And hopefully share a few private moments in her office. He found himself getting hard just thinking about it.

He emerged from his office, paperwork in hand, and looked down the barn to make certain things were going as they should. Carol was standing at Tangerine's stall door, talking to the mare, trying to coax her into coming closer. And he caught a glimpse of Gerald slipping out the back door with a bucket. Linda and Kyle were checking the riding schedule.

As he entered Barn B, he paused to say hello to Britany, Kinley's assistant, then moved on down to Kinley's office. She looked up from studying the paperwork on her desk and smiled as he walked in.

He woke up in her bed this morning to a similar smile, which led to the best morning sex of his life. He thought she might be thinking the same thing when he smiled back and her cheeks flushed.

"The boys just came in to feed Buttons," she said.

"Good. Why did they name him Buttons?"

"Because he keeps butting them while they're feeding him. I think Buttons has imprinted on them, and rushes to be petted when they show up before he eats."

"I hope they don't want to make a pet out of him."

She laughed. "I don't think their parents will agree to it going that far."

He moved around the desk to lay the paperwork in front of her and used it as an excuse to brush her cheek with a kiss. "I got the estimate from the security company you called. A wish list and a reasonable list after a few cutbacks."

A shout came from the back of the barn. "Ms. Green—Ms. Green." The pitch of the voice was definitely young, with an edge of panic.

Kinley shoved to her feet while Wyatt was already on the move toward the door.

Tyler and Greg came rushing up to him as he stepped out the office. Every freckle on Greg's face stood out against his pale skin, and Tyler's eyes were wide. "Buttons is all bloody. Someone's hurt him."

Kinley's shocked, "Oh, my God" followed Wyatt as he broke into a run. He thrust open the back door and ran toward the small pasture where the calf grazed. The milk bottle lay on its side just inside the gate, and Wyatt approached the calf, who staggered toward him. His head was bloody, as were his neck and chest. Wyatt jerked his T-shirt off and started toward him.

His stomach turned as he realized where the blood was coming from.

Someone had cut off Button's ears.

The number of animals injured on her property during her seven years of running the stables had been limited to less than two a year. Always before their injuries happened during their owners' rides. To have someone purposely maim an animal... Every time she thought about how painful it must have been for the calf, nausea gripped her and...

She couldn't think about it right now.

She hadn't cried while calling the police, the vet, or while calling the boys' parents to come pick them up and explaining to them what happened. But she could feel it building behind her eyes.

To some, Buttons was just a cow, but to her and the boys, he'd become a pet. He'd begun to recognize them and come to them when they called. The inhumane way he'd been disfigured struck at everything she'd built her life on, caring for animals.

Because the exterior cameras had been disabled by the storm, she couldn't figure out how they could find out who hurt Buttons. But the window of opportunity had been very narrow because the man doing the security assessment had been out there only moments before. Perhaps the man saw someone arriving in the parking lot or hanging around outside.

Finding that out at least gave her something to do. She called the security company and asked to speak to Henry Cima. He was out on a call and they'd have him call as soon as he got back.

She turned her attention to making the next call, one she dreaded. After a second or two, she hit the number on her cell phone and waited for him to pick up.

"Kinley?" Colter's voice was distracted.

"Yes. I want to ask you why you called the other night. You said there's something important you need to talk to me about."

"So, now you want to talk." His tone was snide.

"Someone's been calling me and saying nasty things to me, Colter. Calling me a whore and other things I won't repeat."

Silence hung over the line. "If you think it was me, it wasn't."

"No, I don't think it was you."

"Things are a little hectic right now. The storm damaged a couple of our listings and we're working to get things cleared up. Can I call you back later, say around six?"

"Someone attacked a calf I was keeping here, Colter. They cut its ears off and it nearly bled to death. If you know anything at all, you need to tell me."

"Have you asked that asshole you have working for you?"

"Who?"

"Gary or Jerry."

"Gerald?"

"Yeah. He fucking threatened me the last time I came to the stables."

Gerald. He had to be kidding. Gerald was the most mild-mannered guy she'd ever been around.

Colten continued, cutting off her thoughts. "But someone else did call the other day for an appointment, and while we were viewing a property he asked about you. He said he'd seen us together at a restaurant. He had some less than complimentary things to say."

Her stomach cramped with anxiety. "Who was it?"

"I don't want to say until I check something out. If I give you the name and he has nothing to do with it…."

"Just give me the name and I'll call him myself."

"I can't talk about it right now. My boss just came in."

"Colter. You need to stop jerking my chain. This is important. You need to tell me who it was."

Her answer was silence. He'd closed out the call.

She breathed a frustrated, "Shit."

A tap came on the office door, and at her "Come in," Wyatt opened it and strode in. He'd changed his clothes since she last seen him, bare-chested holding his wadded T-shirt over the calf's head to try and stem the flow of blood.

He took a seat in front of her desk. "I had a talk with the staff. They've agreed to keep what's happened to the calf quiet. That might buy us a few days, but once the police report is released, the newspapers will pick it up."

She knew the reprieve wouldn't last long, and that they might have some clients pull their horses. But she couldn't think about that right now. "Has Dr. Culver left?"

"No. He'll come by to discuss it with you before he leaves."

She studied his face in concern. "Are you all right?"

"Yeah." That brief word didn't say much, but his tight, angry expression spoke volumes. He was upset, possibly as much as she was.

"It could have been Wagner, but because the cameras are down, we'll never know," he said.

"The man who was here doing the estimate left just before it happened. I thought he might have seen someone outside. Maybe someone pulled into the parking lot. He's supposed to call me back when he gets back from his next appointment."

"Good."

"I called Colter and asked him why he wants to talk to me. I told him about the phone calls I've been getting. He said someone had been bad-mouthing me at the real estate office."

"Who?"

"He wouldn't say. Then he said he couldn't talk because his boss walked into his office, and promise he'd get back to me at six."

"Did you tell the officers who came about the phone calls?"

"Yes. They're going to get back to me on that. Every time I get one of those calls, the number is blank. So he's blocked his number, and I know there are numerous ways of doing that."

"The phone company will be able to figure it out."

A headache pounded at her temples, and she yanked off her baseball cap and then the scrunchie holding her pony tail. She dug her fingers through her hair, then leaned her elbows on her desk and rested her head in her hands.

"How were the boys and their parents?" he asked.

"Upset. Even injured, he was coming to them when they called." She closed her eyes against the surge of emotion. "How's Buttons?"

"He's in some pain. Doc Culver sedated him, numbed him up, and stitched the wounds. It doesn't look pretty, but the bleeding is stopped. Doc and I got him back inside and in his stall."

"Did you find...his ears?"

"No. Whoever did it must have taken them with him."

The emotions she'd suppressed shoved up and spilled over, tears streaking down her cheeks in a rush. She clapped a hand over her mouth to hold back the sobs.

Wyatt started up out of his seat, but she threw up a hand and shook her head. She was grateful when he waited for her to regain control. If he touched her, she'd lose it. She took several deep breaths, and then reached for a tissue from the box on her desk. "I've spent my whole life rescuing, rehabilitating, caring for animals, and to have one attacked and disfigured in my own backyard.... Why would anyone harm a harmless calf?"

"Because he's a sick fuck and it makes him feel more powerful. Or someone is very angry with you." He leaned forward in his seat. "Have you pissed anyone off lately?"

"No. Well, Colter, but he wouldn't know the first thing about using a knife on an animal. His weapon of choice is his lying charm."

"I'd suggest Wagner, but he had no way of knowing the calf was even here."

"Unless someone told him." She looked up, once again composed. "He hasn't been back since the day you filmed Tangerine in her stall, has he?"

"No."

"It wasn't the boys. They'd never have hurt him," she said.

"No. Whoever did this has hunting skills and is fast. The window of opportunity was narrow. I was out there at two with the security guy, and I left him to wander around the place after we talked about the placement of the cameras front and back. While he worked up the estimate in his van, he might not have been able to see the calf, but he'd have heard him bawl in pain while it was happening.

"When the technician came back to the office with the estimate, I walked across to show it to you. The boys showed up during that time.

"I think whoever it is cut Buttons just before they went out. The calf would have lost more blood if he'd been standing out there for a while with those injuries. And no one heard anything."

"With the fans going inside, it's impossible to hear much of anything happening outside the barn," she said.

"Agreed. I can't believe any of the staff were involved. They'd have no reason to do it." He shook his head.

Something Colter had said came to mind. She'd think about it more later. She rose. "I'm going down to see Buttons."

She noticed Wyatt started to say something, but quickly backed off. "He's still pretty groggy."

"I just need to see him." She was aware of Wyatt's hand on the small of her back while they walked down to the calf's stall. Buttons' head was wrapped in partially bloodstained bandages. Dr. Culver was standing at the open stall door, the wrinkles around his eyes and mouth deepened by his solemn expression.

"You can unwrap his head tomorrow. I just want to keep up the pressure against the sutures in case there's any further bleeding," he said. "And I don't want him to butt his head against anything."

"I understand."

"He'll be a little disoriented because I've had to cover his ears with the bandages, and he won't be able to hear clearly."

"Okay." She walked over to where Buttons lay on the woodshaving bedding and knelt next to him. The calf's eyes were open, but he still looked a little shocky, and so vulnerable. She stroked his face and let him smell her scent. He bawled softly. She felt like bawling herself. "When will he be able to eat? He hasn't had anything since early this morning."

"I'd hold off for a few hours until he's thrown off the effects of the sedation. He may eat or he may not, depending on his pain level. I'll leave you some medication to give him. I've given him an antibiotic injection that should last at least a week."

She turned her face away as tears broke through her control.

She wiped them away and got to her feet. "Thank you, Dr. Culver."

"I'm sorry this has happened, Kinley." He gave her arm a squeeze.

"I am too." Her control wavered again, and she sucked in another deep breath.

"If there's anything else I can do, let me know. I'll be back to take the stitches out in eight days." He bent to pick up his kit.

"Thank you."

She watched as he walked down the barn.

"Kyle and I are going to work on the exterior security cameras on Barn B and see if we can get them back up until the new ones are installed. The ones on Barn A haven't been affected."

"Thanks. It will put my mind at ease while the horses are out."

He nodded.

She caught his arm. "Please be careful, Wyatt."

He slipped his arms around her and tucked her in against him. She ignored Brittany and Linda's looks from down the barn and rested against him, trying to just relax and soak in the support. When she pulled back, he tucked a strand of hair behind her ear. "Buttons is going to be okay, Kinley. Everything will be all right."

She nodded, but she didn't believe it. A knot of anxiety seemed lodged just beneath her breastbone. She went back to her office, but every nerve seemed to be on edge. To get away from the barn, she jumped back into the daily work, saddling Indira to take out a group of tourists. By the time she and the group got back, she felt calmer. When the last employee left at six, she locked the door with a feeling of relief. As an extra precaution she changed the codes on the doors to Barn B and texted them to Wyatt.

She went to check on Buttons. He was on his feet and bawled at her for attention. For the first time since his attack, some of her pain and worry eased.

CHAPTER 16

WHILE SHE WAS fixing Buttons' bottle, Wyatt came into the storage room. "Did you get the cameras working again?" she asked.

"Not yet. Kyle and I checked the hardware, and it looks good. I'm going to check the breaker and see if it was thrown or partially thrown. The system might have taken a hit."

"Do Morgan and Kyle feel okay about staying tonight after what happened?"

"Yeah. They're okay. Because of the rain predicted later, there won't be many riders coming in, if any. Morgan's in my office cramming for a Trig test. And Kyle's working on a chemistry project."

"Good. I'm going to give Buttons this bottle, then I'll come back over in a couple of hours and give him some feed." She set aside the bottle. "Will you stay with me tonight, Wyatt?"

He straightened from his position against one of the shelves and ran a hand down her arm in a soothing gesture. "Of course."

She'd never been clingy, but the calf's injury was so brutal… "Let me get this done, and then let's go to the house for dinner."

When she let herself into Buttons' stall, the calf walked slowly up to her. She offered him the bottle, and he grabbed the big nipple and tugged and pulled at it without the usual butting. It was easier to force her emotions back now he was feeling better, so she could focus on feeding him and giving him comfort.

Wyatt appeared at the stall door. "I pulled the breaker to the cameras, then reseated it and threw it. They're running now. How's he doing?"

"He's not his usual rambunctious self, but he's eating."

She glanced up at him. "Do you hunt, Wyatt?"

WYATT HAD HOPED they'd never have to have this conversation. He'd been trained in the SEALS to distance himself and look at the adversaries they fought as targets or tangoes. The enemy were always armed and dangerous, so having a choice hadn't really played into it.

"In the teams I was considered an expert marksman. I've always taken that responsibility seriously. I've used my weapon in defense of myself, my teammates, and others who were in danger. The terrorists, drug dealers, and other bad guys I dealt with were armed and willing to kill me and anyone else who stood in their way.

"After all that... shooting defenseless animals for sport just doesn't appeal to me. In fact, the other night when Buttons' mother broke her leg I hung back while Randal dealt with putting her down."

The compassion he read in her expression relieved him.

Her cell phone rang, and he moved into the stall to take over feeding the calf while she answered it.

"It's the police," she said while she swiped the face of the phone to answer the call.

She left the stall to talk to them. From his vantage point, Wyatt watched her pace up and down, listening more than talking. Pausing outside the stall door she said, "I have to go into the station tomorrow and sign some paperwork to give them access to my cell phone and home phone."

Buttons finished the bottle and he gave the calf a pat. "He doesn't seem in pain right now. The time Doc Culver gave him his pain meds is written on the time sheet. I'll come over and give him the next shot in a few hours."

She glanced at her watch. "Colter said he'd call around six, and it's past seven now. I'll give him a call when we get to the house."

By the time Wyatt had scrubbed Buttons' bottle clean and set it on a shelf in the storage room, Kinley was ready to leave. Everything was quiet as they locked up Barn B, and the parking lot was empty except for Wyatt's and Morgan's vehicles and Kyle's motorcycle.

Wyatt got his go-bag from the car and climbed into the golf cart with her to ride over to the house.

Kinley seemed to want to shake off everything that happened and made a salad while he put pork chops and sliced sweet potatoes on the grill.

After dinner, Kinley shooed him outside to relax while she cleaned up. He settled in the glider at one end of the deck and breathed in the lingering aroma of grilled meat and the sweeter fragrance of the clematis growing on the trellis attached to the deck. The small, white, star-shaped flowers clustered in heavy clouds over the edge of the railing.

He'd never allowed himself to dream of having anything like this. He'd lived day to day, never knowing when he'd be called to duty. Now he'd been in one spot for a few months—had his own place and had found a woman who had true feelings for him… Who wasn't screwing him because he was a SEAL… Or was just out to have a good time… Or calling him or emailing him to break up while he was deployed—he could allow himself to think about having something permanent.

Kinley emerged from the house and wandered down to him, a glass of iced tea in each hand. "I tried calling Colter back and it just went to voice mail." She offered him a glass, pulled her phone out of her back pocket and laid it on the small table next to the glider, and sat down. He stretched out an arm along the back behind her, and when she curled against his side, he pushed the seat into a gentle rocking motion. They fell into companionable silence.

"Feeling better?" he asked after a few minutes.

"Yes." She looped an arm around his waist. He curved his arm around her.

She stroked his chest. "You went above and beyond today."

"Just doing the job, boss."

"I don't think some of the things you did today are in the job description I gave you."

He smiled. "Probably not, but when you work on a ranch, you learn a wide range of skills, and you do what's needed." He gave her a gentle squeeze and set the wooden glider in motion again.

When her phone rang, she sighed and sat up to reach for it. "Hey, Shelley." She rose to pace the deck. "I was going to call tomorrow. It's been a rough day."

He watched her expression and knew immediately news had already begun to circulate through the area.

"He's going to recover, but it was pretty traumatic for the poor little guy, and all the crew. How are *you* feeling?"

She paused for a moment, then walked to Wyatt and held out the phone. "Shelley wants to say hello."

He took the phone. "Hello, Shelley."

"Hello Wyatt. I just want say hey and ask you something."

"Sure, what is it?"

"Do you have my girl's back? I mean really have her back?"

"Yeah, I do."

"Good. I want you and Kin to come to dinner one evening."

He was surprised to find he was interested in doing that. "Sure. I'd like that. Just set it up with Kinley."

"Okay. I'm glad you're home, Wyatt. And there's just one other thing."

"Yeah."

"You break my girl's heart and I'll have your balls to hang on my Christmas tree."

He thought about the last few days and smiled. "She's safe with me, Shelley."

"I'm glad to hear that."

He handed the phone back to Kinley.

When Kinley wandered back into the house to finish the conversation, Wyatt tilted his head back and closed his eyes. He couldn't predict the future, but he took nothing for granted that had happened between him and Kinley. The sex was fantastic, but that was only a small part of what was building between them.

But right now wasn't the time for him to try and decipher his feelings.

Instead he turned his thoughts to everything he'd seen and done throughout the day. He ran through when and where he saw each man who worked in Kinley's barns. A man was responsible for Buttons' injuries. Women in his experience were a little squeamish about getting up close and personal with a knife. Buttons' attacker had twisted his neck until he was forced down on the ground. He'd found the bloody, trampled spot and took pictures with his phone, just as the police did.

Once the calf was down, the guy had hacked off Buttons' ears in two quick moves, so his knife had to be sharp as a razor. None of the women would have had the strength to hold down a calf that weighed a hundred-plus pounds to do all that. It had to be a man.

Kyle Stahl was with him cleaning up at the time, and checking the cameras on B barn. Collin Dantz, the other full-timer on Kinley's team…quiet, a little chunky, but good with the horses…didn't seem like a hunter any more than Morgan Baumann the part-timer on his team. Morgan came in after his classes ended and stayed to help riders who came in after work to tack up. Morgan and Collin were busy cleaning the water troughs.

There hadn't been any strange cars in the parking lot. It could have been someone trespassing across the pastures, but the chances of that were slim. Some clients had been out riding, and a tourist party was doing a ride. Those riders could have come upon the scene at any moment.

A sick feeling settled in the pit of his stomach. It had to be someone who was aware of all those things. But he hadn't seen anyone with blood on their clothing or their shoes, other than him. Could they have avoided that while they held the calf in that head-down position? Possibly.

The only one he didn't know about was Gerald. Why was he leaving Barn A with a bucket in his hand? What was in it? All the horses had been put out to pasture. Gerald was supposed to be in charge of Barn A while Wyatt worked on the cameras and the cleanup.

The calf was housed in Barn B and pastured outside that structure. Everyone who'd responded to the boys' shouts came from Barn B. As Kinley said, it was nearly impossible to hear anything happening outside from inside the barn because of the fans.

The hairs rose on the back of his neck. Gerald had been with Kinley for six years. Why would he do something like this?

He heard the back door open and opened his eyes.

"Are you going to sleep in the glider?" Kinley asked with a smile as she approached him.

"No, just thinking."

"Did you bring your clothes in from this afternoon? I can put them in the wash."

It was telling that she was still thinking about the details of the event, just as he was.

He got up to go inside with her. "I threw the T-shirt away, but I need to wash the jeans. If you can put them in to soak, I can turn them on to wash after I get back from the barn later."

"Okay."

He went into the bedroom where he'd left his bag and pulled them out of his duffle. There was dried blood on the cuff of one leg and down the side of the other.

Gerald hadn't had blood on his shoes or his pant legs. If he'd been behind the calf's head holding it down as he cut him, the blood wouldn't have gotten on anything but his hands. The grass was still wet from the storm. Could wet grass have washed the blood off his shoes? And he could have cleaned his hands that way as well.

He needed to talk to Kinley about her relationship with Gerald. But it had already been a helluva day. She'd been dealt a blow both emotionally and professionally. This could wait until tomorrow. They both needed rest.

He sat down on the bed and waited for her to return. A few minutes later she appeared at the door, phone in hand. "The police called from Colter's phone, asking if I was family, then asking me explain the message I left him. I told them about the phone calls here and how someone had been saying things to him about me. It seems he met a client after hours and the man attacked him. He was beaten and had to be taken to the hospital."

Wyatt searched her face. She looked concerned but not overly upset. "Do they have a suspect?"

"The officer said they have a suspect but haven't made the arrest yet. He wouldn't give me the name since it's an ongoing investigation."

His brows jerked up. "We'll know by morning. It'll probably be on the morning news." He caught her hand. "I'm ready to call it a day. How about you?"

"Yes."

"It's nine, so I'll go over and give Buttons his shot."

"I can come with you," she said, but she looked exhausted.

"No reason to do that. It'll only take me a few minutes."

The night air held a hint of more rain and the jasmine planted along the front side of the deck. The closer he got to the stables, the stronger the smell of grass blended with a faint odor of the compost center behind the machine shed. He made a mental note to have some of the hands turn the pile so the fresh manure and wood shavings would degrade.

He left the golf cart and keyed his way into the barn. The night lights inside cast dark shadows over much of the interior. Only two of the horses came to the stall doors, and he gave them both a brief pat and strode down to the storage room. He flipped on the light, retrieved a syringe and the medication the vet left for Buttons, and then drew up the shot and moved on to the stall. The calf lay in the bedding and he gave him a brisk rubbing to sooth him before plunging the needle into his shoulder, then rubbed the site to alleviate any discomfort. After checking the calf's water and putting a small helping of grain in a bucket for him, Wyatt left the calf eating and went out the back door.

It was on the drive back to Kinley's house a thought came to him. What if the bucket Gerald carried contained grain to coax the calf to him? That idea seemed more probable. But how could he prove it? They had at least a hundred buckets of the same type. Within any given day they used nearly half. Frustration tightened his shoulders.

Living with this suspicion while he worked with Gerald was going to be a fucking shit show. He'd install some cameras inside the storage room and stagger them down the central aisle. And he'd pay closer attention to the man's movements. That was about all he could do. Unless he could trick the guy into showing his true nature.

When he let himself in the back door, the house was quiet. He checked the front door and turned off the lights as he wandered back to Kinley's bedroom. Curled on her side atop the covers, she'd undressed and put on an oversized T-shirt to sleep in and climbed onto the bed.

He stood for a moment, taking in the curve of her cheek and the strand of blonde hair that followed its contour to curl beneath her chin. A wave of tenderness struck him. His eyes settled on the shell-pink contour of her ear, only a little lighter than the nipples hidden under her T-shirt. The thought heated his body with more basic needs.

He didn't have to see her naked to grow hard. He'd fallen in lust before, but damn, he never had it this bad. He knew she cared about him as he did her. It was too soon for it to be more wasn't it? But the powerful jumble of emotions he'd experienced for her…This constant need to be with her was telling him something else.

Realizing he was still standing there watching her like a peeping tom, he stepped away from the bed and went across the hall to the main bath to shower.

The warm water eased the tension in his neck, back and

shoulders. He shampooed his hair and, for the tenth time in the past four weeks, reminded himself to get a haircut. He soaped himself with body wash and turned to face the water. He caught movement behind the frosted glass of the stationary shower panel and turned as Kinley, naked and beautiful, stepped in behind him.

Desire avalanched through him, his earlier thoughts having primed his need.

SHE'D NEVER GET enough of Wyatt Taylor. She could look at him for hours. His wide shoulders, his back, his ripped abs, his thighs—and his impressive erection. He was beautiful. The look in his gold-tinted eyes grabbed her by the heart and snapped her forward. She reached for the body wash. "Turn around and I'll wash your back." She squirted the soap down his spine, then, using her hands, spread it into lather over the strong width, then ran her hands down over his tight ass. He braced a hand against the wall but reached back for her. She aligned her body with his and rubbed her breasts against him, pressed in tight, skin-to-skin. Putting her arms around him, she splayed her hands over those wonderful abs and felt them tighten. Touching him was as big a turn-on as him touching her. The empty ache of need made her legs weak. Her breathing came in short, choppy gasps.

Wyatt turned, and she ducked beneath his arm. Water cascaded over them both, rinsing away the soap and splattering her face, but she ignored it. As she cupped his erection, holding it loosely, caressing, running her hand up and down, his mouth took hers with a wild, unfettered hunger.

He backed her out of the shower. They staggered across the hall to the bedroom, leaving behind slippery footprints and a running shower.

Soaking wet and crazed, they tumbled onto the bed and reached for each other. Their bodies came together in a rush, the ebb and flow of their movements frantic. Pleasure swept Kinley up and over too quickly, too intensely, and she climaxed. The answering evidence of Wyatt's release throbbed inside her.

Wyatt fell over onto his back and lay still, catching his breath.

She felt boneless and totally spent. When he grasped her hand, she turned her head to look at him.

His eyes held a light of humor and something else. "If that had been any better, I might not have survived."

She laughed.

"Somebody's going to have to go turn off the water. Rock, paper, scissors?"

She laughed again and balled her hand into a fist. "Let's do it."

CHAPTER 17

WYATT SIPPED HOT coffee while he watched the six o'clock news. The news anchor's voice droned on about an accident on one of the major interstates, no fatalities.

At the flash of Colter Frank's picture on the screen, Wyatt called Kinley's name. She left off packing their lunches and came into the living room. The female newscaster's voice droned on, "A local realtor in the area was assaulted during a meeting at his office. Colter Franks, thirty-one, was found by a colleague in the lobby of the real estate office, beaten and unconscious. His attacker has since been identified as local attorney Hunter Wagner." A picture of Wagner popped up. "Wagner works for the firm of Wagner, Scott, and Hammons."

"While attempting to serve an arrest warrant at Wagner's home, sounds inside the garage led police to the discovery of another crime. Two dogs were found in the garage, caged and in critical condition. They were transported to a local vet for treatment of burns, broken bones, and neglect. Charges against Wagner have been filed for two counts of animal torture and cruelty, a federal crime, and one count of assault and battery against Franks. Other charges are also pending. A warrant for his arrest has been issued.

"Police are urging anyone who sees Wagner to keep their distance and call the number listed below."

Kinley's shocked expression mirrored what Wyatt was feeling. "He's had a full-out meltdown," he said. "Or, if he hasn't, he'll be in panic mode because his secret is out."

"Those poor dogs." She was silent for a moment. "Colter was lucky he wasn't killed."

"Yeah."

"Should I contact the police and tell them we're boarding Tangerine?"

"It might be a good idea."

"I have to go in this morning at eight to sign the paperwork for them to run a trace on the calls. I'll ask to speak to someone about the animal abuse case while I'm there, and I'll get Brittany to cover for me at Barn B. If you could email the video file to my account, I can send it to them if they ask for it."

"Okay. I'll do that as soon as I get into the office." With Wagner at large, the urge to go with her to the station was strong, but he needed to be at the stables, too. And she'd be at the police station surrounded, by cops.

He caught Kinley's arm as she started to turn. "You need to be extra careful, Kinley. The first time Wagner was there, the way he spoke to you made me uncomfortable. If he'll beat a dog and a man, he won't hesitate to do the same, or worse, to a woman. Had he asked you out or anything?"

"No. I shut him down hard before he had the opportunity. I told him I don't date my clients. You saw how he was. Arrogant. Demanding. Disrespectful. The idea that he'd even think that any woman would be attracted to that is beyond me."

"He's still holding a grudge because you did that. Guys like him take every rejection and slight as an attack on their ego. Be vigilant, okay? And you might want to mention all of what you just told me to the cops."

"I will, I promise."

Frustration gnawed at him. "What about taking one of the other employees with you? You can spare Collin for a couple of hours. I'll help with the feedings at Barn B in his place."

She searched his face. "Okay, I can do that."

Fuck. He might as well bite the bullet and clear the board. "What's your relationship with Gerald like these days?"

She looked away for a minute. "He came to me the other day and asked to be transferred to Barn B after a few more weeks. I told him no, and that I need him where he is."

"You know what I'm asking, Kinley."

"I know. There's never been anything romantic between us because I don't have that kind of feelings for him. I thought by keeping him at Barn A while I'm at Barn B would make things more comfortable for us both. He's too good a worker for me to just let him go."

She was too nice for her own good. And a little too trusting. "The separation of being in one barn while you're in the other isn't going to change his feelings."

"I know. But I've never given him any reason to believe my feelings are going to change. And I've had no cause to fire him. He's never pushed."

"But he has made himself invaluable to you to keep you from letting him go."

"I suppose so. But I didn't string him along. I've been walking a tightrope with him for so long, it was a relief when I moved to the other barn."

"Someday you'll have to deal him, Kinley." If the cops didn't do it first.

"I know." She drew a deep breath. "But not today."

"You never slept with Colter Franks, did you?"

It was more a statement than a question. Her gaze leapt to his face. "No!"

"Why not?"

"He wined and dined me, took me for long drives and to a movie or two, and it was nice. He talked a good game. But there was always something... a little too slick about him. I'm denim and he's silk. So I knew we weren't really a match, which made me wary. When I finally figured out that he didn't really want me, but my grandparents' property, I was...furious. Luckily my pride was hurt more than anything else."

"And if you'd slept with him?"

"I'd have had to kill him."

Wyatt laughed and slipped his arms around her to bring her in close. She snuggled against him. When Kinley's cell phone rang, she sighed and reached for the phone in her back pocket. The screen read *no number*. She looked up at him, put the phone on speaker, and pushed the button. "Hello."

"Whore."

She didn't respond, and the silence stretched for several seconds. He'd hung up.

She closed the call and said, "I really hope they can trace the number."

"They will, Kinley." He hoped it wouldn't be too upsetting for her when they did.

THEY ARRIVED AT the barns at six. The parking lot was empty but for Wyatt's SUV. While Kinley keyed in the code for the front door of Barn B and disabled the system, he walked around the perimeter, looking for any kind of disturbance.

His attention stalled on the small pen Buttons had been confined in during the attack. The calf hadn't had enough space to escape. Damnit.

He entered B Barn from the back and went in to check on Buttons. He was bawling and shaking his head, in obvious pain. Kinley stood at the stall door filling the syringe for his injection. She opened the door and stepped in. He tried to butt her, but she sidestepped, turned, and jabbed the needle into his shoulder. As she massaged the site, Wyatt wondered how many shots she'd given in the past seven years to be so adept at giving one to a moving target.

"The boys will be here in a while to feed him. Everything looks okay outside."

"Good. I'll be leaving as soon as we have the morning feedings done. You can go on to Barn A."

"I'll stay until some of the others get here."

Her lips tipped up into her *you've done something I really like* smile that made him want to go all alpha male, carry her off somewhere, and make mad, passionate love to her. He tugged her close and kissed her. At the sound of the front door opening, he released her with a sigh.

"You know we're not fooling anyone. They know we're seeing each other."

"Probably, but what we have is between us, and this is your place of business."

Collin and Brittany came in together and started the feedings. Greg and Tyler arrived, and after a quick, "Morning Mr. Taylor, Ms. Green," proceeded into the storage room to make up Buttons' bottle.

He turned back to Kinley. "Text me when you leave for the police station."

"I will."

On his way out, Wyatt walked down to make certain Buttons' medication had kicked in. Greg and Tyler came down with his bottle. The two teenagers spoke to the calf as they opened the stall door, and he ambled forward to meet them, rubbing his face on Greg's blue jeans-clad leg in a sign of affection.

"Buttons, dude! Now I've got cow slobber and snot on my pants," Greg complained. Tyler laughed and gave the calf a rub. After a rueful shake of his head, Greg joined in.

He was going to regret ever bringing the calf here. With every passing day the emotional wrench of the eventual separation was going to be hard for the two kids.

He went out the back door and jogged over to the other barn, where Gerald and Carol were measuring out the feed for the horses.

"Did you see the news report about Mr. Wagner, Mr. Taylor?" Carol asked.

"Yes, I saw it this morning."

Her round, pleasant face was taut with anger. "I think it explains a lot about Tangerine's behavior."

"I agree, Carol. I need you and the others to keep an eye out for Wagner while you're here. If you see him on the property, close and lock the doors and call the police."

"We will," Carol said.

Once in his office, Wyatt emailed Kinley the video file and tried to settle into updating some of the files. When he caught himself glancing at his watch for the second time in half an hour, he shook his head and got to his feet.

He needed to do something physical to keep his mind off things. The compost shed would be a good place to start. He got a shovel and a rake from the storage room and sauntered out the front door. He was halfway to the golf cart when Carol stepped out and called to him. He beckoned to her.

"There's something I need to talk to you about," she said as she reached him.

"Why don't you come with me, then? I'm just driving over to the compost shed."

Carol got in, and he pulled up to the gate. Carol got out and opened it for him to drive through, then closed it and got back in. He drove around past the practice circle and Barn B, and turned left through the pasture. The fifty feet or so beyond Barn B was a shed that housed a tractor and other farming equipment. Along the far side of the shed, and built of four-by-four posts sunk into the ground and one-by-six boards of treated lumber was the compost center. It was called a shed, but looked more like sections of wooden fencing put together to create a sixteen-foot-long structure open on one side. It was where the many pounds of horse manure, grass clippings, and mulched leaves and limbs were brought and dumped. Sections of PVC piping had been inserted into the center of four separate piles to circulate air into the decomposing matter.

The compost was turned every five days and watered periodically until it turned into a rich, black compost they used on the flower beds across the front of the barns. Fancying the area around the structures was mostly for the clients, but he'd also seen clients buying the compost for their own flower beds.

He thought of it as Kinley's pet project, but it was useful, cost nothing to do since they'd be dumping the grass clippings, manure and leaves somewhere anyway, and it was bringing in a small profit.

He pulled to a stop in front of the shed and shut off the engine. Resting an elbow on the steering wheel he turned to look at Carol. "What is it you want to talk about?"

"I've been thinking about this since yesterday. I've worked here for five years. I love my job, and I really like the people I work with. Most of the time. That's what makes this so hard."

When she paused, he interjected, "You're not quitting are you, Carol?"

"No. Oh, no." She laughed but it had a nervous, stressed edge to it.

"Good, I'm relieved. You're great with the horses and the clients. You'd be damn hard to replace."

She teared up a little. "Thank you so much for saying that. I love my job. Love working with the horses." She drew a deep breath and seemed to regain her composure by staring straight ahead. "Mr. Taylor... I think Gerald may be the one who hurt Buttons."

CHAPTER 18

THE POLICE STATION was a one-story, sprawling building with careful landscaping and the American flag fluttering overhead. White patrol vehicles with either Police or Sheriff written on the sides in distinctive cobalt blue print were scattered throughout the parking lot.

Kinley parked the truck next to one of the patrol vehicles and turned off the engine. In the eight years she'd lived in Fredericksburg, she never had any reason to visit the structure.

"Do you think they'll ever figure out who cut Buttons' ears off?" Collin asked. His buzz-cut blond hair framed his wide, handsome face, making him look younger than his actual age of twenty-two. He was taking a year off from college to earn enough money to go back in the fall and finish his degree.

"I don't know. I hope so. But I'm here to notify the detective in charge of Hunter Wagner's case that we have Tangerine on our property. And I have to sign some paperwork for another issue."

"Does this other issue have any connection to the other two?"

She'd never thought of that possibility. Or had she? In fact, every time she thought about it, she got a sick feeling in the pit of her stomach. "I honestly don't know. And it isn't some deep, dark secret. I just haven't wanted to talk about it. I've been getting obscene phone calls. A man calls me and calls me names. And says other things."

"Shit, I'm sorry, Ms. Green."

"The police are getting involved, and I hope they'll be able to track the guy down and arrest him." She opened the car door. "Let's go in and get this behind us."

"Okay."

Collin took his duty as escort seriously, and stayed close by her side as they walked through the parking lot and into the building. Signing the paperwork took only a few minutes, and she was given a number to call when she needed to speak to the detective in charge of the Wagner case.

"What do you plan on taking at college this fall?" Kinley asked as they got back in the truck to drive back to the ranch. With her nerves stretched taut, she didn't want to talk about any of the things she'd just taken steps to deal with, but couldn't bear the silence either.

"I'm finishing up on my welding courses, and then I'll be doing electrical work."

"What do you plan to do once you graduate?"

"I'm going to move to San Antonio or Dallas and see if I can hire on with one of the big construction companies building developments and businesses, that kind of thing. Think I could somehow arrange my work schedule with you around my classes this fall?"

"Wait until you get your schedule, and let's see what kind of work schedule we can figure out. We're at capacity in both barns, so I'll definitely need the help."

Once on the rural route home, they lapsed into silence. Collin turned to look behind them. "Ms. Green, you know that fancy car Mr. Wagner drives?"

"No. I've never noticed what kind of car he drives."

"Well, I think it's behind us."

Kinley looked in the rearview mirror. It was a beautiful sports car, sleek, and metallic gray, but she couldn't see the driver for the glare on the windshield.

"Can you see the driver, Collin?"

"No. The sun's too bright."

"Keep looking. We can't call the police until we're certain it's him."

"How many Mercedes Coupes could there be in this town?" Nerves stretched his usual laid-back tone to impatience.

Not many, she'd bet. "Okay, call 'em."

"Better to be sorry than have to deal with a violent asshole, right?" Collin said as he dialed the number.

WYATT DIDN'T WANT to lead Carol to any conclusions by sharing his thoughts. "What makes you think Gerald hurt Buttons?"

"When you walked over to take some paperwork to Kinley, he slipped out the back door with the bucket from stall twenty, and he never brought it back. The reason I know is because when Linda and Morgan started evening feedings, the bucket was still gone, and I had to go get a replacement for it. We stencil the numbers on both sides of the buckets so we know which horse it's for. It's more convenient, so we can measure out ten at a time and not get them confused. But you know that." Her hands trembled as she tucked her chin-length hair behind her ears.

"Maverick always leaves a little grain in the bottom of his bucket after the morning feeding. I think he likes to save it for a snack later. We know he does that, so we don't pour it out, but just put the evening feeding on top. He usually cleans his bucket sometime during the night."

At any other time, he'd have chuckled at the idea of a horse saving some of his food for a midnight snack...but this time they were dealing with a brutal abuse of a calf.

"I think Gerald used that grain to get Buttons to come to him. Another thing is...Gerald carries a knife on his belt. I'm sure you've seen it. He sometimes uses it to cut open the bags of feed, cut rope, and other things. It's wicked sharp."

She looked up, her bright blue eyes were tear-glazed. "Do you think I'm totally off base, Mr. Taylor?"

Wyatt ran his hand over the steering wheel. "No. I don't think you're off base at all, Carol. I also saw Gerald go out the door with that bucket, and I've had much the same thoughts."

She looked torn between relief and a crying jag.

Wyatt rushed to say, "That's why we're here."

"It is?"

"Yesterday we searched the area around both barns, and found nothing. But no one searched the compost pile because it's hidden behind the machine shed. I'm going to turn the compost and see if there's a bucket with Buttons' ears in it buried in one of the mounds. Want to be my witness?"

Her jaw firmed. "Yeah. Sure."

Wyatt studied the four large piles of vegetation for any sign of disturbance. The farthest pile looked like it had a recently-turned area. He pulled his leather work gloves out of his back pocket, put them on, then grabbed the shovel out of the back of the cart.

While Carol watched, he started at the edge of the pile, working slowly. A painful cramp ran down into his left two fingers, and he had to stop for a moment, opening and closing his hand until the cramp eased.

"Would you like me to do the digging, Mr. Taylor?" Carol asked.

"No. Just a cramp." He dug deeper into the heart of the pile, and the dull silver rim of the bucket and part of the handle came into view.

"Carol, do you have your phone?"

"I never go anywhere without it." She whipped it out of her back pocket.

"I need you to take pictures of this while I uncover it."

"Sure, Mr. Taylor."

Using his glove-covered hands, he eased the mulched leaves, twigs, horse manure and grass clippings off the top of the bucket, then picked off a stem with a cluster of leaves stuck to it. The inside of the large pail was streaked with dried blood, and a pair of bloody gloves and the two ears lay in the bottom. Though Wyatt was expecting it, seeing them like that ratcheted up his anger, and he took a step back. "While you take pictures, Carol, I'll call the sheriff."

"Okay." She stepped forward and leaned over the bucket and looked inside. Tears ran down her face, and she bit her quivering bottom lip. She seemed to struggle for a few minutes, but shook it off, wiped the tears away with her fingertips, and dried her hand on her jeans. Blinking away more tears, she raised the phone and started taking pictures.

Wyatt tugged off his leather gloves, tossed them in the back of the golf cart, got his cell phone out, dialed the non-emergency number and asked to speak with the sheriff who responded to the original complaint.

The guy was patched in from out in the county. "Leave the bucket where it is, and we'll come over to retrieve it. We'll be about an hour."

He couldn't stand out here all day waiting for them. He and Carol had already been out long enough. Clients would be coming in in droves soon.

"If we leave it and he comes over here to get the bucket, what then?" Carol asked when he told her what the sheriff said.

"We'll both keep an eye on him until they show. You up for that?"

Her eyes sparked with a glint of anger. "Yeah. I can do that."

They drove back to the barn in silence.

"HE'S STILL FOLLOWING us," Collin said.

She could see him in the rearview mirror and didn't need a play-by-play. "He's obviously coming to Silver Linings. We'll just have to deal with it until the cops get there." Thoughts raced through her mind. What if he had a weapon? What if he attacked someone? It was Saturday, and Barn A would be busy. Weekends were always all hands on deck, because so many of their clients wanted to ride on the weekend.

If Wagner did anything aggressive, Wyatt would step in—he wouldn't be able to help himself. And if something happened to him… she'd never get over it. Never. Her heart pounded so hard in her throat that she could hardly breathe.

She pressed her foot on the brake and slowed down, planning to creep along to give the cops time to get there. Maybe they'd be in the parking lot by the time they arrived.

The driver behind them blew his horn. She ignored it. This was a winding county road, so she could go as slowly or as fast as she wanted. The car whipped around her truck and took off like a bullet. Hunter Wagner was behind the wheel.

Kinley swore and stomped on the gas, speeding after him. "Call or text Wyatt and warn him Hunter Wagner is headed to the stables."

A STEADY STREAM of riders began at ten. Most clients dealt with their own tack, but a few needed help, and Gerald was usually the one who provided it. Just watching him handle the horses put Wyatt on edge.

Now he'd seen the bucket and the ears, he didn't want the man anywhere near the animals. He'd broken trust with the animals in his care, as well as everyone he worked with.

He and Kinley had both fielded too many concerned calls from clients and spent too much time laying their fears to rest. But he couldn't be completely certain as long as Gerald was on the premises.

If he could butcher a calf, what would keep him from tampering with the feed or water? It would only take one horse getting sick, injured, or dying, and the exodus would start.

As soon as the last rider cleared the back door, things quieted down and Wyatt walked down to check the stalls that still held horses. There were only five, and their owners would be in shortly. The rest were out to pasture grazing.

The phone rang, and Wyatt went in his office to answer it. It was another client requesting their horse be brought in from the field so they could ride. He'd do it himself, but he needed to keep an eye on Gerald.

Coming out of the office, he asked Linda to go out and get the horse. Since Indira stood saddled and ready, Linda mounted her and rode out.

Gerald wandered to the back door and leaned a shoulder against the door frame. Wyatt walked down to join him.

"Where did you and Carol get off to this morning?" Gerald asked.

The urge to poke the bear hit Wyatt. "We went up to the compost shed and turned some of it. It's coming along, and should be ready to use in a couple of more weeks."

Gerald narrowed his eyes as he looked off into the distance, and there was tension in every line of his body. "I could go up and work on that later."

Wyatt kept his tone easy. "It'll keep till Monday. We're busy today."

As he looked toward Barn B, a string of seven horses and riders, with Kyle in the lead, came out and headed east. He hadn't heard from Kinley since she left at eight thirty. Linda rode back with the horse, dismounted, tied Indira's reins to a ring the farrier used, and took the horse back to its stall.

His phone chirped that he was getting a text. Thinking it was Kinley, he brushed his fingers over the screen to read it. Sensing movement toward the front of the barn Wyatt turned to look in that direction and muttered an oath. The warning on the screen had arrived too late.

Hunter Wagner walked through the open front door, bold as brass, and luckily strode right past Carol, who stood frozen just outside the storage room.

Wyatt took a second to assess him. He was wearing a dark blue sport coat, white shirt, and khaki pants. He looked like he was dressed for a business meeting rather than a criminal on the run. But his hands were fisted in the pockets of his coat. The possibility that he might have a weapon was foremost in Wyatt's mind as he said, "Step into one of the stalls and call the Sheriff's department, Gerald." He paused beside Linda. "Take Indira over to Barn B, see if they need any help, and stay there until I text you." She nodded, untied Indira's reins, and rode back out toward Barn B.

Now that all but two of his people were out of the way, he strode over to meet Hunter.

He greeted Wagner before he ever reached him. "Hello, Hunter. Are you here to see Tangerine? She and the filly are out in the small pasture."

Up close, Wagner looked less composed. A fine mist of sweat shone on his face, and his eyes shifted from side to side. "Yeah, I'm here to see my horse and the baby."

"I'll take you out to the pasture."

"No, I want you to go out and bring her in."

Glad for a reason to send Carol out, Wyatt nodded to her. He kept his tone even and relaxed. "Go out and bring Tangerine in for me, Carol."

"Sure, Mr. Taylor." She gave them a wide berth as she got a lead from the wall outside of Tangerine's stall and walked out the back door. Wyatt beckoned to Gerald as he came out of the stall. "Go with Carol and help her with the foal, Gerald."

With the barn empty now, he and Wagner waited side by side. "Why do you want to see Tangerine, Hunter?"

"I may not have a chance to see her again for a while. She and I have some unfinished business."

He didn't like the sound of that. A sound from the other end of the barn caught his attention and he turned to see Kinley and Collin at the front door. Fear for Kinley sent prickles racing from the crown of his head down his spine and his heart hammered in his throat. Kinley could not be near this. He waved them off.

EVERY INSTINCT IN Kinley's body demanded she grab whatever weapon she could lay her hands on and go to Wyatt. But he'd put himself in harm's way to protect her. So instead, Kinley stepped back out of sight and beckoned Collin to do the same. A patrol vehicle pulled into the parking lot with the sheriff's logo across the side. Her heart beat so hard she could barely catch her breath as two men in uniform exited the vehicle. She ran down the sloped sidewalk to them before they got within view of the open barn door.

"Hunter Wagner's inside," she announced. The two of them automatically reached for the weapons and drew them. "Wait! Wait. I have people in there. My stable manager, Wyatt Taylor, is in there with him. And I don't know where my other people are."

"I'm Deputy Fischer and this is Deputy Decker. How many people?"

"We always have four full-time hands and one supervisor in each barn during the weekend." She rattled off the names. "I think Wyatt is trying to talk Hunter down. They were standing together talking, and Wyatt gestured for us to back off."

Why hadn't she called ahead to warn him sooner? He could have locked the doors and kept Wagner outside. Tears burned her eyes.

One of the deputies touched her elbow. "You're talking about Judge Taylor's son."

"Yes."

The two exchanged a look. "We've met him before. He can handle himself."

That was what she was worried about. Wyatt believed there wasn't a problem of any kind that he couldn't solve. "He can't against a bullet," she said, her voice hoarse with emotion.

"Did you see a weapon?" Decker asked.

"No. But we're talking about a man who tortures animals. And he's standing there, probably demanding to see the horse we board for him. A horse we suspect he's abused the way he did those poor dogs. The only reason he'd want to see her is to hurt her, and since Wyatt won't allow him to do that..."

"Wagner will probably try to kill her," Decker said.

"Yes. Besides my employees, and Tangerine, there are other horses in there too."

"Are the front and back doors the only exits?"

"No. There's a door that leads into our feed storage room from the outside."

"Take Deputy Fischer to it and let him in. I'll go around back to the other door after I notify dispatch what's going on here and call for backup."

"No sirens," Fischer said. "We don't want to panic him."

Decker nodded.

Kinley beckoned to Collin. "Collin, go over to Barn B and tell them we're under lockdown until further notice. Have Brittany radio anyone on a tourist ride to keep everyone out on the trails until we call them in."

Collin sprinted toward the other barn.

CHAPTER 19

HUNTER WALKED TOWARD the open back door and stared out toward the pastures. "How do you stand this day after day?" he asked.

"It's better than being cooped up in an office dealing with assholes all day," Wyatt said.

Hunter laughed, but there was a wild kind of desperation in his tone. "Fuckin-A!"

Gerald came around the corner with Tangerine in tow.

"Where's the baby?" Hunter asked.

"Carol stopped to let her drink some water at one of the troughs. She'll be here in a minute."

Tangerine's hooves clattered as she stepped inside on the concrete floor. Gerald walked steadily toward them.

Six feet away, Tangerine started dancing wildly and pulling back on the rope. Gerald braced his feet and held on.

"Hey, Tangerine." Hunter shook free of the left sleeve of his jacket. "Remember the love bite you gave me the last time we were together?" He held up his arm to show a large, deep half-moon scar on his left forearm. "I can't really leave anything undone now I'm going away." He shook free of the right sleeve and dropped his jacket on the floor.

Already tensed for action, Wyatt saw the pistol in his hand at the same moment Hunter aimed his weapon at the horse.

Wyatt lunged against him, and shoved Hunter's arm down. The weapon discharged, and the bullet ricocheted into the wall. Tangerine screamed and reared, her front legs pawing the air. She broke free of Gerald's hold, and he dove out of her way as the frightened horse galloped toward the other end of the barn.

Wyatt shoved Hunter back against the hard wooden wall of the closest stall and wedged his weak arm under Hunter's chin, putting all his weight behind it, hoping to choke him out. Hunter gagged and choked, but still struggled to turn the barrel of the gun on him. Wyatt shoved the barrel of the gun up and head-butted Hunter in the nose. Hunter yelped, and Wyatt jerked the weapon out of his hand and hit him in the side of his head once, then twice. Hunter slumped and, thinking the man was done, Wyatt released him and backed away.

The front door slammed shut, and Wyatt's attention snapped toward the sound. Faced with a closed door, Tangerine reared again, and for a moment he thought she might tumble backwards, but she pivoted on her hind legs, dropped forward, and ran back toward him.

Hunter staggered to his feet, his nose bleeding, shaking his head as though to clear it.

"Stop, Hunter," Wyatt yelled.

Hunter took one step, then two, toward him, putting himself directly in Tangerine's path. At the last second, he turned to face her and opened his arms, as though he meant to embrace her. She swerved to avoid him, but hit his arm. He screamed as the arm snapped back and the blow spun him around so he landed facedown on the concrete floor with an audible thump.

Every drop of thoroughbred blood in Tangerine's body was evident as she ran out into the pasture, her mane and tail flying, the lead rope dragging behind her.

Wyatt knelt by Hunter. He was still breathing, but unconscious. He looked up as Deputy Fischer ran up from the other end of barn, his weapon drawn.

"Are you okay?" Fischer asked.

"Yeah." Wyatt offered him the pistol.

Fischer holstered his weapon and took it gingerly by the grip with two fingers, then returned his attention to Hunter. "You disarmed him?"

"Yeah."

"I'll get a statement in a few minutes, after I call an ambulance." He stepped aside to use the radio on his shoulder.

Deputy Decker came in the back door, weapon drawn, but holstered it when he saw his partner calling for an ambulance.

Wyatt looked up as Gerald came to stand over Hunter.

"Tangerine had the last word," he said.

"Seems so," Wyatt agreed and got to his feet.

Gerald studied his face for a long moment. "You protected everyone here and stayed behind to deal with him."

"It was the right thing to do." What he'd been trained to do.

Gerald nodded.

They both turned at the sound of running feet from the other end of the barn. Kinley rushed to Wyatt and, gripping his shirt, checked him for injuries. She raised a hand to touch his forehead. "You have a red spot. Did he hit you?"

"No, we kind of bumped heads. I think my skull's a little thicker than his."

Deputy Fischer snickered, then coughed.

As the fear cleared from her expression, tears followed, and when she buried her face against his chest, sobbing, and held onto him, he cupped the back of her head and held on too.

Carol came to the door and peeked in. "Gerald's heading toward the compost pile, Mr. Taylor."

"Shit!" The asshole slipped away while he was distracted.

He looked down at Kinley. He'd hoped to have just a little while to explain everything to her. "Deputy Decker, we have another situation. I'm going to need you to go with me."

"Fischer, you got this?" Decker asked.

"Yeah. I'm waiting for the ambulance. And there's another unit on its way."

KINLEY FELL INTO step with the two men. Whatever was going on, she refused to be locked out again to worry and be terrified that something might happen to Wyatt.

"You don't need to go with us, Kinley."

"My property, my business."

Wyatt shook his head. "Whatever happens, stay back. Gerald carries a very large, very sharp knife."

"I know. For ranch work. He uses it to cut rope, feed bags, whatever he needs it for."

"He used it for something more yesterday."

Her heart seemed to drop into her stomach. She'd hoped... No she'd pushed the thoughts and feelings away. She hadn't wanted it to be true. After six years, she wanted to believe in the trust she'd given him.

Wyatt's tawny eyes held a light of sympathy as he touched her arm. "You drive." He lowered the small tailgate on the golf cart and hopped up to sit on the back of the cart.

Feeling numb, she got into the driver's seat and started the engine while Deputy Decker took the seat next to her.

Wyatt slid up behind the seats so he could explain the situation to the deputy. "We have a calf we've been keeping for a few weeks. Yesterday someone cut off his ears."

"Shit!" Decker muttered in disgust.

"Carol Pointer, one of our workers, had a suspicion of who it was and spoke to me about it this morning. We were missing a feed bucket from Barn A. She saw Gerald Hawbecker take it yesterday, but he never returned with it. We found it in the compost pile behind the equipment shed this morning with a pair of bloody work gloves and the calf's ears in it. I called your office, and they were supposed to send someone to come this morning to get it, but they haven't shown up."

Decker swore again, then asked, "You're sure this guy has a knife?"

Kinley answered. "He carries one for work in a sheath on his belt. But up to now, at least with people, he's never been violent." She added, gripping the steering wheel harder. "He has no history of violence that I know of, and has never been arrested."

Gerald had wanted to hurt her and her business because she didn't love him. Not the way he wanted her to. He'd known exactly where to strike to cause the most damage.

Gerald came into view as they rounded the equipment shed. He held the bucket by the handle. As they came to a stop, he froze, his arms out to his sides, the bucket dangling from his fingers.

Decker got out of the cart and drew his gun, but held it at his side as he approached Gerald.

Wyatt got out of the cart and moved to stand next to Kinley, his hand resting on her shoulder.

"Put down the bucket, Mr. Hawbecker," Decker ordered.

When he complied, Kinley released the breath she was holding.

"I'm arresting you on suspicion of animal cruelty, Mr. Hawbecker."

Gerald nodded and put his hands behind his back. The deputy holstered his weapon, cuffed him, then removed the knife from his belt.

Kinley slid free of the driver's seat, leaving it empty for the deputy. Decker guided Gerald to the passenger seat. Once Gerald was seated, the deputy released the right cuff, threaded it around the front bar supporting the cart's roof and cuffed his right hand again.

"I'll send someone back up to get you," Decker said as he set the bucket in the back of the golf cart. He got behind the wheel.

Wyatt took her hand. "We'll walk. I think both of us need a few minutes."

Decker's gaze strayed to Kinley, and he nodded.

Gerald finally broke his silence. "I'm sorry, Kinley. About the calf… about the phone calls."

His admission about the calf was painful enough, but she flinched when he confessed to the phone calls. She couldn't look at Gerald and maintain her composure. The hurt ran too deep for words. She thought she knew him, but she couldn't have, if he was capable of all of this.

As the golf cart disappeared around the equipment shed, Wyatt turned in the opposite direction and started walking toward the house with Kinley.

Kinley's mind felt dull, and her emotions numb with shock, but she still had to deal with the barns. She got her cell out and called Collin to tell everyone the lockdown had been lifted, and instructed him to radio Kyle and Brittany that it was safe for them to return to Barn B with their tourist groups.

After she returned her phone to her back pocket, Wyatt guided her hand through his arm as though they were taking a stroll.

She rested her head against his arm. "You don't always have to solve every problem, Wyatt. I knew you'd be the one who'd deal with Hunter."

"It's what I was trained to do, Kinley. And it was my responsibility to keep our people and the clients who come to Silver Linings safe."

"I know." His SEAL training was as ingrained in him as his DNA. She needed to accept that. "I knew he'd be armed, and I was terrified he'd kill you." She turned to cling to him for a moment.

"He was never interested in me. He wanted to kill Tangerine. She'd bitten his arm. He called it unfinished business."

"God."

"The chance of something like this happening again are slim."

She shook her head at his attempt to comfort her and turned back toward the house again. They walked in silence for a few minutes.

"I'm sorry about Gerald," Wyatt said.

"Did you know he was the one calling me?" she asked.

"Not for certain, but I suspected it might be him. I was trying to warn you this morning when we talked about him."

She nodded. "I didn't want to believe it was him. Colter said he threatened him when he came to the stables when we were dating. I never saw that side of him."

All the things that had happened since Wyatt had come to

work for her, and all they'd experienced since they were together, played through her mind. They were almost to the house when she tightened her grip on his arm and pulled him to a stop.

"I was terrified for you, Wyatt. I knew if something happened to you, I'd never get over it." Tears glazed her eyes. "I love you, Wyatt. I know it's too fast. Too soon. But the way you were with Katie that day, and the first time we made love... and so many...firsts..."

He turn her to face him, cupped her face and kissed her. "...and morning sex, and the way you smile when you're thinking about what we've done together."

She drew him down for a kiss before he said something really embarrassing.

He grinned when they came up for air, and his tawny brown eyes held a light that made her knees weak. "I knew when I was watching you sleep last night. You make me feel things I've never felt for any other woman, Kinley. I love you."

How could she help but love him when he said things like that?

He caught her hand and smiled. "Besides...we're a good fit."

She groaned. "You're never going to let me live that down, are you?"

He chuckled. "Nope. Never. Just keep walking, and we may reach the house and have enough time to double-check that before Fischer and Decker show up, asking for our statements."

"I think we'd better hurry." She broke into a run and shot him a grin over her shoulder.

Wyatt ran after her and caught her hand. Every step he took with her reminded him he'd finally found his way...to laughter, and love... to a new life beyond what he'd lost. And he was ready for it.

FOR MORE INFORMATION ABOUT TERESA REASOR

Website: www.teresareasor.com

MILITARY ROMANTIC SUSPENSE
BREAKING FREE (Book 1 of the SEAL Team Heartbreakers)
BREAKING THROUGH (Book 2 of the SEAL Team Heartbreakers)
BREAKING AWAY (Book 3 of the SEAL Team Heartbreakers)
BREAKING TIES (A SEAL Team Heartbreakers Novella)
BUILDING TIES (Book 4 of the SEAL Team Heartbreakers)
BREAKING BOUNDARIES (Book 5 of the SEAL Team Heartbreakers)
BREAKING OUT (BOOK 6 of the SEAL Team Heartbreakers)
BREAKING POINT (A SEAL Team Heartbreakers Novella)
BREAKING HEARTS (Book 7 of the SEAL Team Heartbreakers)
BREAKING CHAINS (Book 8 of the SEAL Team Heartbreakers)
BUILDING STRENGTH (Book 9 of the SEAL Team Heartbreakers)
BUILDING FAMILY (Book 10 of the SEAL Team Heartbreakers)
BUILDING COURAGE (Book 11 of the SEAL Team Heartbreakers)
Coming Soon!

SEALS IN PARADISE SERIES
HOT SEAL, RUSTY NAIL
HOT SEAL, ROMAN NIGHTS
HOT SEAL, TAKING THE PLUNGE
HOT SEAL, MIDNIGHT MAGIC
HOT SEAL, OPEN ARMS

PARANORMAL ROMANCE
TIMELESS
DEEP WITHIN THE SHADOWS (Book 1 of the Superstition Series)
DEEP WITHIN THE STONE (Book 2 of the Superstition Series)
DEEP WITHIN THE MIND (Book 3 of the Superstition Series)
coming soon
WHISPER IN MY EAR

HAVE WAND, WILL TRAVEL SERIES (Box Set)
HAVE WAND, WILL TRAVEL (Book 1 Have Wand, Will Travel)
ONCE BITTEN, TWICE SHY (Book 2 Have Wand, Will Travel)
ADVENTURES OF A WITCHY WALLFLOWER (Book 3 Have Wand, Will Travel)

HISTORICAL ROMANCE
CAPTIVE HEARTS
HIGHLAND MOONLIGHT
TO CAPTURE A HIGHLANDER'S HEART: THE TRILOGY

The Highland Moonlight Spinoff Trilogy in parts
TO CAPTURE A HIGHLANDER'S HEART: THE BEGINNING
TO CAPTURE A HIGHLANDER'S HEART: THE COURTSHIP
TO CAPTURE A HIGHLANDER'S HEART: THE WEDDING NIGHT

SHORT STORIES
AN AUTOMATED DEATH: A STEAMPUNK SHORT STORY
CAUGHT IN THE ACT: A HUMOROUS SHORT STORY

CHILDREN'S BOOK
WILLY C. SPARKS, THE DRAGON WHO LOST HIS FIRE

Made in United States
Troutdale, OR
01/22/2024